CANYON ROAD

by

Thea Thomas

Books by Thea Thomas

The Canyon Road Love Stories series:
Canyon Road
One Love
Two Weddings

YA:
The People in the Mirror

Dark Urban:
Amethyst Dreams

CANYON ROAD

by

Thea Thomas

Canyon Road
Thea Thomas

Emerson & Tilman, Publishers
129 Pendleton Way #55
Washougal, WA 98671

All Rights Reserved
No part of this publication may be reproduced, distributed, or transmitted
in any form, or by any means, including photocopying, recording,
or other electronic or mechanical methods, without the prior
written permission of the author, except brief quotations
in critical reviews and other noncommercial
uses permitted by copyright law.
This is a work of fiction.
Names, characters, places, and incidents are fictional.

Book & cover design by Emerson & Tilman

Canyon Road
Copyright © 2014-2018 Thea Thomas/Emerson & Tilman

Paperback ISBN: 978-1-947151-40-6

[1. FICTION/Romance/Contemporary
2. FICTION/Contemporary Women
3. FICTION/Romance/General] I. Title.
BIC: FM
First Edition

DEDICATION

For all those who believe

That the well of Love springs eternal

Chapter 1

A Rescue

Sage hated driving the limo on the Canyon Road at night—it was unwieldy on the sinuous road. She heard the echo of motorcycles behind her and hoped she'd be in her driveway before they caught up to her, but just then the cycles came roaring over the hill.

She slowed. She didn't want them to see where she lived. The motorcycles surrounded her, the drivers jeering and taunting. "Hey, guys! Look at that gorgeous babe!" A sandpapery voice shouted beside her as she pushed the button to roll the window up.

Sage's hands perspired in her black driving gloves, but she refused to stop, though they had slowed her to a crawl.

"She's mine!" The abrasive voice close to her went on. "First dibs."

"Cool it, Dutch! We ain't into that," a huge bulk shouted from the other side of the limo. "We just wanna teach these sorts they don't own the roads."

"Aww, come on Bull-Man, let me have me fun!"

Sage couldn't see through the mass of high-beam head-lights as they circled her, and she suddenly felt the car slipping as the motorcycle gang guided her car into the ditch. She slammed on the brakes and heard a thud and a curse as one of them drove into her from behind.

"What's the matter?"

"She don't wanna go into the ditch," Bull-Man said. "She wants to keep taking up the whole road. We might have to push her."

"Hey—a car's coming!" one of them shouted.

"Clear out!" Bull-Man commanded.

They roared around her and continued on down the road as if they'd only smiled and waved as they passed.

Sage gripped the steering wheel, shaking to her core, sweat on her brow, yet numb with cold. As the roar of the motorcycles faded, the clatter of a sports car came up from behind.

She tried to back the limo away from the edge of the ditch, although its back end already straddled the road. She realized she was forced with the decision whether to roll into the ditch or stay put and perhaps get broad-sided. Ditch, she decided, which would avoid hurting someone else.

The approaching car coughed and sneezed as it crested the hill behind her. It wasn't coming too fast— she'd sit tight.

She turned and watched the dark hilltop.

*　　*

Michael missed his country life. Especially today he'd ached to see the moon in an open sky, stars brightly twinkling without the dimming, dulling city lights. He wanted to feel the wind through his hair, as if his very thoughts could be cleared out though the strands of his hair.

He hadn't taken his vintage MGA out on the road for some time, and tonight felt like the perfect time to clear out the cogs for both the little, old car and himself. He drove to Canyon Road, feeling proud of himself for escaping the city routine for a couple hours. But instead of peace of mind, the MGA gave him no end of trouble on the hills. He'd have to rebuild the carburetor—again!

He crested the hill, wondering if the car would even get him home, when he saw in the darkness a white limousine stretched across the road like a beached, albino whale.

He slowed, then coasted slowly toward the limo, stopping thirty feet away from it. He flashed his high beams. The limo flashed its high beams. He rolled a little closer, cautious, unable to see through the tinted glass.

Then he pulled over onto the shoulder, got out and walked around the limo. Altogether strange. he knocked on the driver's side window, thinking it was not a smart thing to do.

The window rolled down a small crack.

"What's going on?" He still couldn't see the driver.

"Oh ... the motorcycles, and the ditch ..." a woman's voice whispered.

"The motorcycles, the ditch ... well, that's clear. What's the idea?" Michael gestured broadly in imitation of the limo stretched across the road. "Are you a suicidal chauffeur?"

"No. I'm not ... I'm ... ahhh ...."

Michael felt his frustration rising. Just a couple hours of peace and quiet, just a simple drive in the country—was that too much to ask? "Do you suppose you could roll the window down a bit? Maybe that would help us approach something resembling conversation."

There was a pause.

"I'm ... afraid," a quivering voice finally responded.

Michael melted. "Don't be afraid, I'm going to help you. Your car is in a dangerous position. If someone with a car that can actually get over that hill comes up on you, it could be ...."

"Yes, yes, you're right," the voice from inside said. The window hummed down.

Michael was unprepared for the stunning features of the anonymous woman faintly revealed in the hollow darkness of the quarter moon light. Dazzling white blonde hair escaped from a black silk scarf wrapped tightly about her alabaster face. Huge pale blue eyes checked him out with mistrust, but softened, taking in his tousled brown hair, the studious horn-rimmed glasses.

"I'm trapped," Sage said. "When I let go of the brake to give it gas, it rolls farther into the ditch. I'm afraid to try again. I'm going to roll nose first into the ditch. I'm so shaky now, I don't know which end is up."

"No, no nose first for you. Put on the emergency brake and get out."

"Get out?"

"Yes. If it does go nose first, no point in both of us going with it."

"I see, yes." Sage pulled on the emergency brake and got out. Her knees buckled. She grabbed the door. Michael reached out and steadied her.

"Sorry," Sage apologized. "I was really frightened. I'm usually tougher."

"Just be calm." Michael led her to his MGA and gave her a hand into the passenger seat.

He went back to the limo, put it in reverse, revved the engine and popped off the emergency brake. Throwing gravel, he pulled the limo back onto the road. That was too easy, he thought. What's this woman doing driving a limo if she doesn't know how? She must have gotten the job with her looks.

Well, it was none of his business. If his personal philosophy held up, it just meant he'd done a good deed and now his car should at least get him home. He pulled the limo onto the shoulder and walked back to the MGA.

"Do you think you can drive now?"

"I don't think I'll drive for a month!" Sage said.

"Hmmm ..." Michael said, wondering about the extent of this good-deed-of-the-evening. "Well ...."

"Oh! I see what you're saying," Sage smiled up at him. What a smile! "But this is my driveway right here. Do you think you could drive this beast up to the house?"

Michael let his eyes wander up the three-quarter mile long drive. "Well, sure. Okay. Will it cause any problems if I leave my car here at the edge of the drive?"

"Problems? Why would it cause problems? It'll cause problems if you don't and someone runs into it."

"Right. I just meant, if anyone else was coming into the driveway and my car is sitting in the way."

"No one's coming at this hour."

"Good." Michael escorted Sage to the passenger side of the limo, pulled it into the drive, then went back and parked his MGA at the end of the drive. Then he climbed back in the limo and drove it up the curving road to the unlighted mansion on the black hillside.

They said nothing on the way.

"Where shall I park 'the beast?'" Michael finally said when they came to the front door.

"Right here is fine. How I hate this thing!"

He turned off the engine and handed Sage the keys.

"Thank you so much!" Sage said, sounding much more relaxed. "I'm awfully lucky you came along. I think you saved my life!"

"Oh, I doubt it, things weren't that out of control."

"If you'd been there five minutes earlier, you wouldn't be saying that."

"There's more to the story?"

"Yes. Believe me, yes!" Sage abruptly changed the subject, "I feel like I need a cup of tea. Would you like some, or coffee, or something?"

"Actually, yes, I'd appreciate that, thanks."

They got out and walked to the front door. Sage unlocked it and led them through the entryway, across a broad expanse of echoing marble as they passed a winding stairway, and finally into the kitchen. Small night-lights lit the way as they approached. Michael could not make out much, blindly following the swish of black silk in front of him.

This chauffeur has privileges, Michael thought.

They came into an open space, and as they did so, blinding white light flooded the kitchen. Michael squinted in the glare of lights and their reflection off of exotic pots and pans, hanging from a network of brass, and what looked like acres of white ceramic tiles.

"Do you want to keep me company in the kitchen, or do you want to sit out here in the living room alone?"

"Since you put it that way, I believe I'll keep you company in the kitchen, of course."

"Good."

Sage flung her black silk scarf and the floor-length black silk cape onto a chair revealing herself in a strapless, floor-length, form-fitting royal blue velvet dress, white blonde waves of hair cascading down her bare back to her waist.

Michael stifled a gasp, glad that Sage had her back to him as she fussed with a tea kettle, not noticing his reaction.

"I'll just put the water on and I'll be right back." She put the kettle on and kicked off her four-inch royal blue heels in one movement. Picking up her shoes, she waved at Michael with them as she bolted from the kitchen.

In her wake the black silk cape fell deftly to the floor. Michael walked over, picked it up and, with a behavior he would never expect of himself, buried his face in its dark softness, into a heady fragrance. He felt himself as shaky as this woman had been the moment he met her. But his reasons were quite different.

He picked the scarf up, folded both the scarf and the cape neatly and sat in one of the straight-backed chairs, holding them in his lap. He was not one to lose his composure. At least, that's what he told himself.

Moments later, Sage came back in the kitchen in blue jeans and chambray shirt, bare-footed, hair caught up in a tortoiseshell shell colored barrette.

"There now, I feel better!" She looked at Michael. "You look ... not better. Why are you holding these?" She took the scarf and wrap from him.

Michael shrugged. "They, uhhh, fell to the floor."

"I see." Sage flung them onto another chair. "So, let's see, I was making tea and coffee." She got out mugs, instant coffee, tea and spoons.

"I think I'll have tea with you."

"Excellent!" Sage turned and extended her hand, "By the way, I'm Sage."

"It's a pleasure." Michael stood and extended his hand. "I'm Michael," As their hands touched, a shock arced between their fingers. They both jumped and giggled.

"From handling the silk," Sage said, shaking his hand. "I'm glad to meet you, Michael." She fussed with the tea, then arranged everything on a tray and brought it over to the kitchen counter where Michael had moved while she made the tea.

"We'll let the tea steep for a minute. Want some sugar?" Sage asked.

Michael shook his head.

"Keeps me sweet," she said. "I'm calmed down now. So let me tell you what happened. A band of marauding motorcyclists accosted me."

"Really?!"

"They surrounded the limo and tried to force me into the ditch. When they heard your car, they roared off."

"So I really did rescue you from a terrible fate," Michael said.

"Yes. You really did."

"I thought you were just an exceptionally poor driver."

Sage laughed. "I'm an awful driver of that yacht-sized thing-in-the-name-of-a-car. Ordinary cars I drive, well, in an ordinary fashion."

Michael studied Sage, bemused with the sensation of familiarity. He knew he had never met this woman, and yet ....

"Did I spill something?" she asked.

"I'm sorry," Michael said, embarrassed. "It's just, you look so familiar, but not quite. I can't put my finger on it."

"I know what it is," Sage said, "but let's see if you can figure it out."

"I don't know. It sounds idiotic to say, 'haven't I seen you somewhere before,' But haven't I seen you somewhere before?"

"It happens to me all the time."

"I'm sure! You're quite ... beautiful."

"You're sweet, but that's not the point ... I happen to have the exact features of someone who had a high public profile."

"Of course!" Michael said. "You look exactly like the singer Cher in her glory days! But your coloring ...."

"I know, my coloring makes it confusing. My mother was Zuni Native American, my father, white blond Southern Californian. I got her features, but came up with the pale recessive coloring." She smiled. "I look like Cher right down to the crossed front teeth." She pointed them out.

"Charming," Michael said. "I've find symmetrical anomalies in teeth quite charming."

"Probably because yours are so perfect. My dentist feels as you do. He said I'd have to go to someone else if I wanted them changed, that they are 'personable' as they are."

"A little bump in stunning beauty is a plus, not a minus."

"Stop, stop, please," Sage laughed. "I warn you, I can be embarrassed!"

They both fell silent.

Sage sipped her tea. "Boy, I needed this ... I can just feel myself relaxing!"

"My cue!" Michael stood.

"Oh no, no, I didn't mean ... oh how rude! I'm not even thinking about what I'm saying. I've ... it's been a difficult week for me. I've not been myself."

"No offense taken, I really do have to get on the road. My car's giving me trouble and I don't want to end up stuck out there all night in the wee hours. Or hours that are more wee than now," he added, glancing at the clock.

"Almost one! My goodness, I had no idea it was that late. You ... you could stay here," Sage said cautiously. "After all, you did just save my life, and you may have noticed there's a room or two to spare."

Michael had a fleeting consideration of Sage's irate boss if he, a total stranger, stayed over night, as well as an irate boss of his own if he didn't get to work on time in the morning.

"Thanks, but no, I've got to get home and get up at five-thirty to go to work. But if I could spend a few minutes looking at my carburetor under a yard light, it'd be a big help."

"Of course. Here ...." She went over to the far wall, flipped a switch, the back yard became flooded in light. "See? Shall I drive you down to your car?"

"No, thanks. You've been through enough, and I don't mind a quiet walk in the country night."

"Okay." Sage stifled a yawn. "Nerves," she said. "I'll just leave this door unlocked. When you're through, you can turn off the yard lights and lock this door. Let me grab you a flashlight." She stepped into the pantry and returned with a gigantic flashlight.

"Well! That ought to light my way!" Michael said, stepping outside.

Sage let out a tiny giggle. "I do hope so! Thanks again, Michael. Good night."

"Good night." Michael walked to his car in the peaceful moonlight, his thoughts on this beautiful, curious woman.

Chapter 2
Sage

Sage woke up the next morning in her darkened room, crying. *"Aunt Vicky!"* she strained to call out in her dream, but the words wouldn't come and the effort woke her up, her face wet with tears.

She climbed out of bed and dragged herself down a long hallway, passing closed doors. At the opposite end she opened a huge dark walnut double door, a crack just wide enough to let herself into the rooms. Heavy pale green draperies and sensual, massively over-stuffed furniture seemed to fill the rooms almost to the dark-beamed ceiling. Brilliant swaths of light came pouring through the parted curtains of the windows and the French doors. A giant walnut four-poster bed stood on a dais dominating the room, and across the room, a natural stone fireplace faced the bed.

Sage stole across the thick creme and pale green Chinese carpet to the mantle. She reached out her hand, like a little bird-wing flutter, toward an array of framed photographs depicting a stunningly handsome woman, with a voluptuous-yet-trim hour-glass body, captured in moments of not-entirely-candid poses— evening gown, riding gear, bathing suit—wearing an inflexible smile less comfortably than the clothing, the poses.

Sage touched the cold face of her favorite picture of her aunt with gentle affection, then turned and left, silently closing the massive door behind her. She went downstairs into the kitchen and filled the tea kettle with water, and flipping it on to boil. A yellow-lined sheet of paper on the white-tile counter caught her eye, and then the memory of last night tumbled like an avalanche into her mind.

The note read:
To the limo driver—Thanks for the yard light and tea. Michael

"You're welcome," Sage said, feeling oddly rebuffed. It *was* a thank-you note, but she wished he'd not written anything, its tone sounded so peculiar and cold, as if this man acknowledged a distance between them that would have been perfectly fine left unsaid.

She balled the note up and threw it in the trash, dismissing it as she poured her tea.

In the breakfast nook she sat staring out at the sunshine and ivy. Well, she *thought* she'd dismissed the note and its author. But there, in her mind's eye, suddenly and clearly, appeared Michael's guileless, sincere face with that winsome tousle of dark auburn hair.

Even when at first he'd been angry and cold, she'd still found him likable. Wind-tossed hair, big brown eyes, a sprinkling of freckles. Thin as a lightning bolt, strong, sure of himself, but shy too. She'd never even met a man who had all the features of ... Michael. Sage smiled. Go ahead, be familiar, she thought. You'll never see him again.

So she let her mind wander over his lean body, his wide strong mouth, straight nose and studious brown ... actually, perhaps almost hazel ... eyes behind the glasses. She didn't realize that his face had etched itself so completely in her mind, but now the morning's bright sunlight faded as she recalled the plane of his cheekbone when she stole a glance at him in the dark limo.

"Anyway, I can't be frustrated with him, he really did save me," she said aloud, watching the wren dancing in the bushes outside the window. Then she realized this was the first waking moment she'd actually taken her mind off her Aunt Vicky in three weeks.

She sighed. The phone rang.

"*Soooo* ... what do you want to do now?" her friend, Tina, asked as if they were in the middle of a conversation.

"Hello to you too! I don't want to do anything."

"Uh-uh, wrong answer. It's time to *par-ty!* We gotta get your blood circulating again, girl!"

Sage giggled. "What are you getting at?"

"Either you start getting in motion or moss is going to grow on you."

"I'm not that bad."

"No, no, she's not that bad," Tina announced to an omnipresent audience, "she's not that bad! When was the last time you went out?"

"Last night!" Sage answered. *"Touché!"*

Tina was quiet for a moment. Then, "oh yeah? What'd you do?"

"I went to an opening at the Newport Harbor Art Museum."

"Hmm. Okay. That's a little more 'out' than going to the grocery store. But who'd you go with? What'd you wear? Where'd you go after?"

"I wore the blue velvet."

"Ohhh! And?"

"And the blue velvet pumps."

"You know what I mean ...."

"And I think it was enough that I got out."

"Okay, okay, you didn't go with anyone, you didn't go anywhere after, you just lugged that awful limo from the canyon to Newport and back again."

"That's right."

"And you're proud of yourself."

"Noooo—not proud, not ashamed. There's nothing to be either about. But ..." Sage got up and started to wander about.

"But? There's a but? But what?"

"Well, I had quite an adventure."

"Really? What?" Tina's curiosity crackled.

"A motorcycle gang tried to steer me off the road."

"No!"

"Yes."

"What *happened*?"

"I'm trying to tell you. I was frightened to death. I really was. It made me ... makes me angry to have been so weak, but ...."

"Of *course* you were frightened. I shudder to think what they would have done to you! So then what?"

"So they heard a car coming and they left."

"That's all?" Tina sounded disappointed.

"A moment ago you were worried about me."

"Certainly. But you seem to be in one piece ...."

"Anyway, that's not really quite all. The limo was stretched dangerously across both lanes of the road, heading into the ditch. I couldn't handle it. I couldn't back it up. I just kept going further into the ditch. Then this sports car came over the hill. A man jumped out, pulled the limo back out onto the road, then drove me up to the house."

"No kidding! How exciting. You weren't afraid of him?"

"No. He was so nice. I mean, at first he was really angry and sounded mean. Then when it was clear that I was helpless—and I *was*, I hate being that way, but there it is—he turned so sweet. So, no, I wasn't afraid of him in the least."

"And then what happened?"

"And, and, and!" Sage exclaimed, "And that's all." Sage found herself in the kitchen, standing in front of the trash. She pulled out the crumpled note.

"Oh." Tina sounded deflated.

"Except he came in and we had some tea."

"*And?*" Excitement again.

"And then he went down and got his car and brought it up to look at it under the yard lights. I went up to bed. I was wiped out and, anyway, he certainly didn't need me hovering over him while he figured out the problems with his car." Sage held the phone with her shoulder and smoothed out the note. "He turned out the yard lights and locked the door when he left. And *that* really is all."

"Hmmm." Tina was silent for a moment—Sage couldn't read her. "You let him have run of all the valuable stuff there, and just went to bed?"

Surprised, Sage retorted, "Stuff? I don't care about this 'stuff.' Besides, he maybe saved my life. He's not the sort of person who takes 'stuff.' "

"*Ohhh*—sensitive. Okay. White-hearted, honest guy. I suppose there's a couple of them left. What'd he look like?"

"He was ... he is sort of ... gorgeous."

"*WHAT?!*" Complete incredulity from Tina. "Sage calls a man gorgeous? Never! Never even 'nice looking.' Who *is* this masked marauder? When do I meet him? What's his name?"

"Michael. You don't meet him. I'll never see him again."

"*Augh!* You meet a man you think is gorgeous, and you know nothing about him!"

"Except that he writes terse notes on yellow-lined paper."

Sage ran her finger over his scribbled signature.

"But why didn't you find out more about him?"

"Last night I was ... I felt weird, confused ... because of the motorcycle gang. So, it was just, he did this good Samaritan deed, and that's all. Then this morning I woke up with a terrible dream about Aunt Vicky."

"Oh, Sage, I'm sorry."

"Well, I'm all right. But, you know. Anyway, and then I remembered him."

"Tell me more about the gorgeous Michael."

"There's nothing more to tell. He's thin, he has a mop of curly sort of auburn hair, sincere eyes, hazel I think, a wonderful mouth, wonderful cheekbones. Straight, perfect teeth."

"Jeez, again with the teeth, Sage! But, anyway, he sounds wonderful. Poor Sage, everything is so ...."

"No, not poor Sage," Sage said. "What the earth-angel Michael did for me was to let me see that I'm still alive, that I can have a pleasant, positive emotion. For a while I wasn't mourning. And, just when you called, I was thinking about him, and realized that again, I had a moment when I wasn't missing Aunt Vicky. And, like I said, he opened the door in me where I remember that I'm still alive."

"Of course you're still alive!" Tina said. "Look at you! You're incredible! You're beautiful, you're intelligent, you're educated, you're talented, you're rich ...."

"No, I'm not."

"Okay, scratch rich, who needs it anyway? But anyway, you're all that and not even bitchy. I mean, you're really sweet and nice. You're the kind of woman women love to hate."

"What a waste of their energy if that's true."

"Well, *I* don't hate you! You're my best friend, and friends like you are hard to find. But now I have a mission. I can do something for *you*, for a change. I'm going to help you find Michael."

"Are you crazy?" Sage folded up Michael's smoothed-out note and tucked it in her pocket. "I've never chased men, and I'm not about to start now!"

"You don't have to, I'm going to do it for you."

"I'm not desperate, Tina." Sage felt peeved.

"That's for sure," Tina answered quickly. "Every man wants you. The point is, you've never been interested in anyone."

"I'm not interested in Michael either. I mean, I don't know anything about him. I just liked his looks and he was kind. That's all."

"Phooey, Sage. Tell me another story! I've never seen you even *look* at a man without there being quite a bit more than his appearance and a first impression."

Exasperating, Sage thought. "It's just exasperating how well you know me, Tina," Sage shook her head in frustration. "But please don't embarrass me by stalking some completely unsuspecting man."

"Well, I *will* have to find him before I can stalk him. First things first." Tina gave a mischievous, rascally, chuckle.

Chapter 3
Michael

Michael sat staring at the computer chip architecture, but he couldn't find the bug. Couldn't see, for that matter, anything but a pair of diamond-sparkling-pale-turquoise-blue-eyes. Why was this strange woman taking his mind, *how* was she taking his mind? Why indeed, he thought, trying to shake the vision of her.

But he couldn't let someone he didn't even know interfere with his work. A woman who looked like that, who lived in a place like that, who wore clothes like that and yet who drove a limo—well, she surely must be living a complicated personal life. And he'd be unwise to get anywhere near it. It was definitely not his style, on the basis of simply knowing her first name and where her driveway was, to chase a woman.

Anyway, she probably wasn't actually as stunning as she'd seemed. And, what's more, since when did he base his opinion of a woman on looks?

True, he continued silently. But no one would overlook her looks. She was as mysteriously beautiful shrouded in the black cape in the dark car as she was shockingly beautiful in the bare-shouldered blue velvet gown, as she was home-spun beautiful in blue jeans, work shirt and bare feet.

But she wasn't just beautiful. He'd really *liked* her.

In the six-months since he came to California he'd gone out with several women. But he hadn't met one that he *liked*. He didn't dislike anyone. He just hadn't—he chuckled, thinking of the shock that passed between them the previous night when he reached out to shake her hand—he hadn't had a shock pass between him and any of those other women.

Yes, something about this woman called to him. Never mind her cover-girl beauty. Her earthy seriousness, and her slightly sad energy attracted him. He wondered where she grew up. There was country-side and heartlands in her somewhere, just as there was in him, transplant that he was. She *had* said her mother was Zuni.

There was a small knock at Michael's door and a pixie face with buck teeth peeked through.

"Busy?" Millie, the mail-girl, asked.

"Does a slave wear chains?" Michael answered.

Millie grinned, exposing more and yet more teeth. She came in and closed the door. "I got some mail for you."

"No kidding? And I thought you just wanted to talk to me!"

Millie rolled her eyes toward the ceiling. "Don't I always, and don't you know it! And by the way, can I take you to lunch today?"

"Not on your salary. But I'll take you tomorrow or Wednesday. Today I don't get to have lunch. I've got to make some sense out of the errors in this chip. What have you got there, flyers about the company picnic?"

"No, that's a ways away yet. This looks real jazzy!" She handed him a square pale grey envelope. "An invitation to something!"

Michael looked at the return. "It's from my uncle."

"Bless your uncle! The saint who got you this job and brought a few moments of happiness into this girl's otherwise dull life," Millie folded her hands in prayer and looking skyward.

"Hmmm ..." Michael said. "Well, the one who got me this job, anyway."

"I reiterate, bless his heart. Or bless him where he wants it. Bless his bank accounts and stocks."

Michael laughed, his furrowed brow relaxing. "You've never even met him, and you know right where to bless him!"

"Yeah, I've met a couple of rich folks."

"I wonder why he sent this to the office?" Michael said, puzzled, still not opening the envelope.

"Because you've moved four times since you've been in California," Millie pointed out.

"Good point." He pulled out the square invitation.

"So what's the occasion?"

Michael looked at the curlicued script. "it's a 'no-occasion dress party.' "

"Oh, come on!" Millie challenged.

Michael handed her the invitation.

"Yeah, that's what it says." Millie gave the invitation back to him. "Anyway ... it sounds like fun," she added wistfully.

"I thought I'd stop by to see my uncle last night, but my carburetor gave me so much trouble I decided not to, but to hurry home, only to come upon a limo stretched across the whole road."

"What?" Millie returned from fantasizing about a no-occasion dress party. "What was across the road?"

"A limousine. Stretched across the road."

"See, that's what I thought you said! What was it doing there?"

"Not the back stroke."

"Corny, Michael."

"Sorry! Turns out the driver was a woman. Apparently a motorcycle gang had been harassing her, trying to get the limo in the ditch when I came along and scared them off."

"Not much of a driver, huh?"

"My thought exactly. In fact, everything about her was pretty curious."

"Such as?" Millie prompted.

"Well, she was driving the limo, but she was the most unlikely limo driver I ever saw. Of course, here in southern California ...."

"So, she was beautiful ...."

"Quite stunning, quite, yes."

"Ugh," Millie said, leaning against the closed door. "I already don't like this story."

"Silly Millie! So let's say she's a limo driver."

"Yes, let's."

"But she walked into the house—I mean, mansion—as though she owned it."

"Into the house? You *did* make progress!"

Michael smiled. "You little conclusion jumper! She was so discombobulated that she asked me if I'd drive the limo up to the house."

"If someone as wonderful as you came out of the night and rescued me, I guess I'd be discombobulated, too! I'm discombobulated, just bringing your mail." Millie perched on the uncomfortable arm of the office chair. "There are times when you get more than one piece of mail, that I think of keeping a piece back, just in case you don't get any mail the next day so I can bring you something every day. Just, you know, the junk mail. Of course, I haven't ever really done it, but I *have* thought about it."

"What a wit!" Michael chuckled.

"Without beauty, I have to make up where I can. Maybe that's something I've got over the beauty you met?"

"Look Millie, you don't have to take a back seat to anybody! You're great, you're funny, you're a good friend, and you have your own beauty."

"Oh, well," Millie answered philosophically, "better friend than foe."

"I should hope so." Michael paused, then went on, "That's another interesting aspect about this woman. After getting over being terrified, she had a light, easy-going nature. Not at all spoiled or even self-centered."

"I hear wedding bells."

"That's just your head ringing from too much romanticizing. I'll never see her again. Anyway, back to this business," Michael pointed at the invitation, "I suppose I'll have to go, although I hate the thought. Maybe you'd like to go? You can help keep me from getting bored, you'll get some incredible food and drink, and who knows, you might even enjoy yourself."

"Really? Seriously? Oh boy! With you I'd enjoy shoveling out a pig pen. Not to compare the two events. I'd *love* to go—as if I didn't already drop a broad enough hint."

"It's semi-formal. Are you okay with that?"

"I'm okay with that, I've got stuff. The preparation is not the problem. Getting the event to occur has been the problem."

"It's nice of you to be so enthusiastic. I hope you won't be disappointed when you're bored stiff. Although I like being with my uncle one-on-one, I don't much care for these sorts of events."

"I'll try and disguise my yawns. Really Michael, this is wonderful. You've made my day!"

"You're too easy, Millie."

"Not as a rule. Well, I suppose we'd both better pretend like we work a bit, huh?"

"True. I've got some pretty serious pretending to do."

Millie gave a little wave as she slid her petite body through the door, running head long into Michael's supervisor.

"Oh, my! You've been working out, haven't you, Mr. Allerton?" Michael heard her say to his boss. He grinned at how incorrigible-but-cute Millie was, and turned his attention back to his work.

Chapter 4
Tina & Sage

Tina roared her little black convertible VW up Sage's driveway.

Sage happened to be standing at the window watching what appeared to be an exotic bug, black with long wild dark hair and a blood-red scarf flailing about in the wind, tearing up the winding ribbon of the drive.

She grabbed a bottle-green scarf and ran downstairs, opening the front door just as Tina shut off the ignition.

"Ready?" Tina shouted as if the engine were still running.

"Sure, let's go!" Sage hopped in, tying her scarf around her head and slipping on her sunglasses.

"We look like Christmas coming!" Tina started up the engine again, pointing to their red and green scarves.

Sage laughed. "Christmas in May! Why not?"

They wound down the driveway and then along Canyon Road, then Tina turned onto a back road among a frenzy of construction on all sides.

"No more natural hills," Sage said sadly.

"Yeah, it's awful. I'm going to miss looking up at the hills and the stars from my little apartment. That was the number one reason I moved into my place, the view of the hills." She waved her hand at the monster equipment, chomping away at the land. "They call this progress."

"That's what makes me so unhappy about losing Aunt Vicky's place, they'll do this to her acres, those lovely mountains. It's only fifteen minutes from here. You know they'll do it."

"You haven't lost the place yet! Don't count little deformed chicks before they're hatched."

"You have such a way with words," Sage said as they pulled up at *Rutabegorz*, their favorite health-food-but-not-like-health-food restaurant.

Inside, seated in a cool private booth, they hunkered down over the menu.

"I'm going to sin," Tina stage-whispered. "I'm going to have a tofu peach shake."

"You deserve it," Sage reassured her. "You've been good."

"I know! I lost five pounds in the last month."

"From where?" Sage asked. "You don't have five pounds to lose."

"I got a hair cut."

"Don't say it," Sage shook her head. "Your hair is wonderful!"

"This from the Hair Goddess."

"I'm serious!"

"Do you know what I'd give to have your hair?" Tina asked.

"Nothing much I hope because I'm pretty attached to it ... ha, ha!"

"Funny."

The waitress took their orders and when she stepped away, there was a cozy lull between the two friends.

Finally Tina said, "you forgot to pack luggage."

"Huh?"

"You went far away, but didn't pack any luggage."

"Sorry," Sage turned her attention to Tina. "I *did* go pretty far away. But the good news is how quickly I can come back now."

"Yes," Tina reached over and patted Sage's hand. "There was no love between your Aunt Victoria and me, but I never wish anyone harm, and I'm sorry that her tragedy causes you so much pain."

Sage stared at her hands wrapped around the glass of water. "I've lost the last person in my life who is family. I feel—unmoored. There's my father's mother. I've met her twice, and don't know her at all. There's my mother's people at the reservation. Maybe that's where I'll go. But now I'm so betwixt and between. I know I can go there, but I don't know if I would stay there—because of how I've changed. It wouldn't be the same. *I'm* not the same.

"I haven't been to the reservation since I was fourteen when I went there to get away from Aunt Vicky. But I felt like I wasn't a part of the people like

I had been only two short years before. My coloring separates me from my people."

"Don't think about it, Sage. I'm your friend, *I'll* be your family. We can get a place together, you can get a job—horrible thought that *that* is."

"I don't mind," Sage protested, "I like the idea of being occupied. But I'm not qualified to do anything but be spoiled."

"Well," Tina said as the waitress placed their plates of delicious food before them, "we both know that's not true."

"What, that I'm not qualified to be spoiled?"

"Yes. No. What I mean, and you know what I mean, is that you can do anything you set your mind to. Not to mention that with your looks you could pick up where your Aunt Victoria left off with her budding actress career."

"That's not for me. I can't act."

"I've seen actresses that can't act. And I've seen you act wonderfully."

"I don't know what you mean by that."

Tina went on, "Not to mention guys like Willie who are just dying to make you happy."

"Oh Tina, please! Mr. Williamson is not 'Willie,' and his interest in me was orchestrated by Aunt Vicky. Neither of us have any intentions toward the other."

"Please, please, *please*, Sage, tell that to anyone, but spare *me!* I never saw so much fire in an old codger's eyes as when he lays them, on you!"

"*Augh,* Tina! Why do I hang out with you?"

"Because I'm honest."

"You don't mince words, that's true, but please be respectful about Mr. Williamson, who is a very nice person."

"Okay! Don't hemorrhage! But there's something funny there, I'm telling you. I consulted everything about him, I wanted to feel at ease about his intentions toward you. I did the I Ching, the Tarot, my pendulum. You remember I read his palm at that party, all tongue-in-cheek. But I was seriously checking him out. Everything about him in relation to you is sort of cloaked."

"I believe I recall you saying he was the most awesome specimen of male human flesh over forty-five you'd ever seen."

"Also true. But body and soul do not always have the same appearance."

"You're wrong about him, Tina, I'm telling you, you're wrong." Sage silently wondered if her friend was jealous because he hadn't given *her* a tumble.

"Well then, I won't say another word about him," Tina said, digging into her food. "The next thing that'll happen is you'll think I'm jealous because he didn't make overtures to me."

Sage poised her fork in mid-air. "Uncanny, Tina. Absolutely uncanny. Sometimes you make me flat-out nervous."

"Bingo! Well, then, Willie, ahm, Mr. Williamson is a closed book."

"No, Tina, there are no closed books between us. I can't hide anything from you, anyway!"

"True."

"But this reminds me—I got an invitation from the now infamous Mr. Williamson a few days ago for a party he's throwing in a couple weeks. I don't intend to go. In fact, I'm upset with him for having a party so soon after Aunt Vicky's death. But anyway … I'll RSVP for you and you can go in my stead."

"By myself? Thanks for nothing, Sage."

"What do you mean?"

"I'm not going to one of those we-all-know-each-other-but-no-one-knows-you events by myself. The thought strikes horror. On the other hand, if we both went, we'd probably have a ball!"

"I'm not in the mood, Tina. Besides, like I said, I want to protest the … untimeliness."

Tina reflected for a moment. "Now don't get angry with me, Sage, but Victoria was your relative, not his. By the time of the party, it'll be two months or so. I know it seems like no time to you, but, life is for the living, as they say. I think you should go, Sage. I really think you *should*. Just to put your mind on other things."

"But I feel so unsocial. And, and, you know, I'd have to face Anthony."

"So now it's Anthony! I can't call him Willie in the privacy of our own luncheon, but you, without a segue, go from Mr. Williamson to 'Anthony!' "

"Of course I call him Anthony. After all, I've known him most of my life and we're neigbors. The point is, I don't want to have to deal with him right now. Not that there's anything … but …."

"Sounds lame, Sage."

"Let's just drop it all, altogether."

"Too easy!"

"Okay, Tina. I'll admit that the word 'marriage' did come up, once. With Aunt Vicky in the room."

"*Aha!*"

"'Aha' all you please. It felt strangely un-natural at the time, it felt staged. But I was shocked, with my Aunt in the room, like suggesting a business deal."

"Yes, Sage, an arranged marriage to join mutual properties and the old guy is getting a beautiful young woman to boot."

"Even *that* I think I could kind of understand. But there was something else, some undercurrent between them."

"Hmm." Tina's brow furrowed.

"I'm sure I read the whole thing wrong, since I was so shocked. I mean, there was nothing for him to base a proposal on. To this very moment we've never even held hands or, or anything."

"Yeah, well, Sage, let's be practical here. You don't want to lose your Aunt Victoria's land, it appears that everything you thought she had is gone in bad investments. You've sold off all the cars except that awful limo because you can't find a buyer, you've had to dismiss the domestic help."

"Yes, Tina, I know all of what I've had to do."

"I'm just saying, don't you think the wise route would be to marry—dare I be familiar?—Anthony?"

"Wise? But Tina, I'm not in love with him."

"Well, that settles that! No weighing things out. No sleepless nights trying to make the best, the most practical decision."

"I did try to give it some serious thought, Tina, but it's just no-go. If I can't do it, I can't do it!"

Tina studied Sage's impassioned expression. "You'll have to face him sooner or later. He's enough of a gentleman not to harass you during your grief. And he won't at a party he's throwing, either."

"You're right. He calls me once a week, and we have polite little five-minute chats where neither of us says anything. I know he's concerned about me. He tried to get me to let his cook stay at my place. I always say no thanks, but every couple of days there's a food package at my door. In his heart he *is* a dear man."

"A dear, good-looking, wealthy, man, who probably loves you. But don't worry, don't give it a thought. You don't love him."

"Well, I don't. Not in that way. I care deeply for him in an … uncle-like way. Anyway, I'm not going to make a life decision based on stress in the middle of my life crisis."

"It might be easier to let him know how you feel— or don't feel—about him, at his party."

"Perhaps. Anyway, if you're there, Tina, I'll feel more at ease."

"See? I'm good for something! Now let me get serious about this food before my peach shake gels."

Chapter 5
Sage

"Then wear something of mine," Sage said to the extremely disgusted reflection of Tina in the mirror. "But, really, that dress is *trés* cute."

Tina, in a pink cotton summer dress, turned to grimace at Sage in a floor length white sheath, with black beading across the shoulders and down one side where a slit in the skirt revealed a well-turned thigh.

"Cute, Sage?! I look like your handmaid."

"I'm probably over-dressed," Sage turned to look at the back of her dress.

"The riddle goes, when is an over-dressed woman under-dressed?" Tina said.

Sage turned around, smiled, and put an arm around her friend's shoulders. "Come on! Let's raid some closets!"

"No, we'll be late."

"I don't care about that, I don't even want to go!"

"I *do* though. But not looking like this!" Tina squinted at her reflection. "Ugh! Nothing helps. What was I thinking? What does semi-formal *mean* to me, anyway?"

"Relax, Tina." Sage pushed her to the walk-in closet. "I guess you're a size or two smaller than me, but I bet we can find something."

"I've always been partial to the blue velvet."

"I just wore that thing."

"When?"

"You remember, that opening I went to, when the motorcycle gang scared me to death."

"That was *three weeks* ago!"

"Yes."

"To me, 'having just worn something,' means it still has body heat in it."

Sage laughed.

"I'm serious, Sage!"

"But with formal things," Sage pointed out, "I don't like to be seen in them more than once a season, if that much."

"Okay, fine. You don't have to wear it again this season. With me in it, no one will recognize it."

"I don't care if you don't care! Here, try it on."

Sage handed the blue velvet gown to Tina.

"Thank goodness I wore this strapless foundation," Tina said as Sage helped her slip it on over her hair. Then Sage zipped it up.

"Looks pretty good back here," Sage said.

"That's half the battle, but things look pretty bad from up here." Tina turned around, the bodice stays were concave where they ought to have been be convex.

"Oh-oh," Sage said.

"Oh-oh is *not* what I had in mind for tonight."

"Turn around." Sage unzipped the back part way, then over-lapped the two sides. She looked around into the mirror.

"How's that? Looks fine, I think."

"Yeah, it looks okay," Tina said. "Titled: 'Scarecrow in Blue Velvet.' I was so proud of losing that weight and now I look kind of spindly. Don't you have any-thing from when you were spindly Sage, say about twelve years old?"

"When I was twelve, I was poor. We're going to make this work. This dress has a little bolero that goes with it. I'm going to baste this together."

"Sew me into the dress? That's one way to make me think twice about doing anything I ought not be doing."

Within half-an-hour, Sage had Tina sewn up into the dress and they were driving the limo through the Williamson gateway, both of them giggling as Sage insisted on carrying out the chauffeur routine to the hilt, getting out and going around to open Tina's door.

Sage handed the doorman her invitation, then she and Tina entered a gigantic circular entry room, three stories high, bathed in a kaleidoscope of colors from the circle of stained glass windows around the dome far above.

"Oh, wow, Sage! *Wow, wow*," Tina stage whispered.

"Excellent word choice, Tina."

"People live like this?"

"People do. You may as well brace yourself. The whole place is fairly ... ah, exotic."

"Wow, Sage," Tina reiterated.

"Are you broken?" Sage edged Tina through the doorway and coaxed her up one of the two circular stairways winding around the walls of the domed entry.

"Where are you taking me?" Tina whispered as they rustled up the stairs.

"To the lady's room. We need to freshen up."

"Oh, yeah, that's right, after all, we just drove nearly two miles and are exhausted and wind-tossed."

"That's more like my Tina," Sage said. "I thought I lost you altogether there for a minute."

"You *did*, for a minute."

Sage led Tina into a massive peach-colored room, walls of peach-tinted mirror, peach carpet, peach ceiling, peach crystal chandeliers.

"Well, Sage, I can't even say wow anymore. I can just die in peace."

"Oh no. You have to see the rest of the mansion, and *then* you can die in peace."

"Look at you," Tina exclaimed. "In that white dress in this peach light, you look like sherbet. I look like mud."

"Will you stop running yourself down? You look fabulous. But I don't need to tell you. You'll see soon enough when all the heads turn."

"As long as you're standing beside me, sure."

"Nope. And I'm going to leave you alone to prove it."

"No, no, don't leave me alone! Anyway, I'm perfectly happy to be the moon to your sun, to glow in your reflected light."

Sage giggled. Strains of classical music came to them at a distance. "Enough poetry, Tina. There's the orchestra, it's a good time to make an entrance."

Sage let the way through a maze of rooms, halls and stairways.

"How do you know this place so well? I'd think you'd have to live here for years to learn your way around."

"I had the head butler take me on a tour once. It's pretty logical when you've been over the whole place."

"I feel like I'm in that Esher drawing where all the people are going up and down stairways that are upside-down and sideways and no one falls off, or runs into anyone. Why do I see so many people far away, but I don't see anyone around us?"

"Because we're going the back way."

Sage went down yet another stairway, closed-in with only a dusky light coming from the noisy room below.

They came out in a huge, bustling kitchen.

"Hi, Robert," Sage greeted a monumentally officious-looking butler.

"Hello, Miss Elgin, I'm glad to see you decided to come, and so will Mr. Williamson."

"Thank you, Robert."

Sage and Tina scooted through the bustle and came out on a patio leading to the grounds that stretched for acres.

"Anthony usually has his throne set up across from the orchestra," Sage said as she moved from the three steps on the brightly-colored patterned tiles of the patio to the terra cotta tiles of the paths on the grounds.

"Sage!" Tina exclaimed, "the pool!"

"Three Olympic-sized pools, actually," Sage noted.

The pools stretched ahead of them out to the fading sunset toward the ocean, each of the three pools tiered three steps below the previous, each cascading a water-fall into the next. One silk oriental carpet after another lined the pools on the terra cotta tiles. Exotic far eastern party lanterns hung about everywhere.

Sage spied Anthony, seated in his usual place when entertaining outside, in a gazebo across from the orchestra.

Chapter 6
Anthony's Party

"I'm a happy man tonight," Anthony said, handing his cell phone to his great-nephew who stood beside his throne-like wicker chair.

"You should be, Uncle Anthony. Everything is perfect."

"It's not just the party that makes me happy, but it's the reason I'm *having* the party."

"I thought it was a no-occasion party."

"That's what the invitations said, only to make sure the guest of honor would come. Robert just informed me that she's here."

"The guest of honor? Who?"

"You'll meet her soon enough." Anthony turned to Michael's companion. "Tell me, missy, are you and Michael an 'item' as they say. Are you serious?"

Millie exchanged a quick look with Michael.

"I'm never serious, I'm just a kidder."

"So he won't come through for you?"

"Really, Mr. Williamson, we're just pals ... from work."

"Tell me something though, am I a prejudiced old man, or is my nephew awfully good-looking?"

"He's *gorgeous*," Millie gushed. She stopped, shy. "Well, that's my reserved opinion."

Anthony laughed. "She's very cute, Michael."

"She is, indeed."

Millie went on, "Michael is not only attractive, he's really smart too! You should hear the things he can talk about. I've never known a man who knew so many things."

"Oh, please, that's enough about me," Michael protested. "Uncle, let me tell you what happened to me on this road a few weeks ago ...."

"Here it comes," Millie said, "the beautiful chauffeur story again."

"Poor Millie, I guess once was enough for you."

"Naa, I'm just kidding. Besides, your uncle might know who the mystery woman is."

"You kids can sure talk a lot about a story without telling it," Anthony pointed out.

"A few weeks ago," Michael began, "I was driving on the Canyon Road. I had in mind to stop and visit you, but my carburetor was giving me trouble, so I decided to head on home. Further down the road was a white limo stretched almost entirely across both lanes. When I walked up to the door of the car, there was this beautiful blonde woman behind the wheel."

"Sage!" Anthony said.

"Oh!" Michael said, then stopped. "So you *do* know her."

"Indeed I do."

"Well, I guess you'd know the domestic staff of your neighbors," Michael reasoned.

"Domestic staff? Sage is anything but domestic staff. What makes you think, what makes you even suggest ...?"

"I assumed, since she was driving the limo ...."

"Oh, I see! That's a reasonable assumption, sure." Anthony laughed heartily. "What a funny picture." He stopped laughing. "But no, it's not at all funny. Why was the limo across the road?"

"Some motorcycle gang had been harassing her. Apparently my arrival was extremely timely, and I scared them off."

"Good for you, Michael! Good for you!"

"That sure answers a lot of questions," Michael observed, "like why she went in the front door as if she owned the place, why she was dressed-up in that blue velvet gown. Of course it doesn't answer why she was driving the limo ...."

"The poor girl has happened on some extremely hard times of late," Anthony said. "It wouldn't be appropriate for me to discuss her personal life, but she's a strong young woman. I've come to admire her more and more in the recent past."

"Speaking of blue velvet, there's a beautiful gown," Millie said, gesturing.

"That's her!" Michael said, surprised.

"But she's not blonde."

"No, I mean the blonde."

"You don't mean the blue velvet?"

Michael looked again. "Well, yes, I believe that *is* the blue velvet, but that's not Sage." Michael brought Millie to her feet, so she could see Sage around the plant blocking her view. "*That's* Sage."

Millie gasped. "Oh, Michael, now I see what you've been talking about! That ... that is not a usual human being."

"No, that's a goddess," Anthony said.

Michael studied his uncle's enchantment at the sight of Sage. So this was where Sage's entanglement was, right in the branches of his own family tree, Michael thought.

*   *

Sage touched her friend's shoulder and gestured to the gazebo, so engrossed was Tina in the pool and orchestra that she couldn't look anywhere else. Sage started to make a little wave to Anthony when her eye caught Michael's. Her hand froze as their eyes met.

"Sage," Tina said, "do you see that wonderful, wonderful looking man there?"

"That's him!" Sage whispered.

"Him who?"

"Michael, that's Michael."

"Oh boy, Sage. Yeah, you'd have to be blind to not call *that* gorgeous. But isn't it a strange coincidence, him being here? Sage ... *Sage?* How long are we going to stand here like we're waving good-by to the Queen Mary?"

"Ahh, yes, embarrassing." Sage moved toward the gazebo, Tina shadowing her.

"Sage!" Anthony exclaimed, standing, taking her hand, kissing her cheek. "I'm so glad you came. Everything else just fades away when you're around. But before I get too faded away, I'd like to introduce you to my nephew, Michael, who, I've just been learning, you've recently met."

"Your nephew!"

"Yes. And Michael was telling me about your recent accidental encounter. Then you appeared, right on cue."

"I have no secrets!" Sage said.

"On the contrary, you are a woman of great mystery. Let me introduce Michael's friend, Millie," Anthony continued.

"I'm happy to meet you," Sage said, finally noticing the small woman in the large wicker chair, "This is my friend, Tina."

"Nice to meet you, Tina. Sage," Anthony said, "Do you mind if I whisk you away for a few moments? I have something I'd like to discuss with you. You don't mind being left with Michael, do you Tina?"

"Of course not."

Anthony took Sage by the elbow. She cast a glance over her shoulder to Tina who was thoroughly engrossed in striking up a conversation with Michael.

"My nephew seems to be a hit with women."

"Oh? Is he a womanizer?"

"No, I think not. On the contrary, I suspect. I suspect he's shy. Well, look at the mouse he's with."

"She's quite charming," Sage said quietly.

"Yes. Quite, *quite* charming. But Sage, I'm not interested in talking about them."

He led her beyond the third pool into a sunken rose garden, and sat with her on a small secluded white bench, trellised about with rose vines.

"I'm so glad you came this evening, Sage."

"I nearly didn't as I'm still in mourning. But Tina wanted to come so badly."

"I'm sorry, Sage. Do you feel this party is too soon?" Anthony studied her carefully, anxiety on his brow.

Sage took in his sincerity, and lost heart to make a criticism. She decided to go with Tina's point that Victoria was not Anthony's relative. "No, it's all right, Anthony. I ... just don't feel much like partying."

"But I'm so glad you're here," Anthony said. "I ah, ahm. I'm stuttering ...."

Looking at Anthony, Sage had to agree with Tina. Excellent physique, a great mass of silver hair, youthful blue, long-lashed eyes—yes, quite attractive. Good looks certainly run in this family, she thought, reflecting on Michael.

"You see Sage, I threw this party tonight for you. I knew you wouldn't come if I told you you were the guest of honor. But ...ahh, I understand this is a hard time for you. I have someone from my staff check on you a couple times a week just to make sure you're all right, but you're a strong young woman and don't want to be treated as though you can't make it on your own. What can I do to let you know I'm here without intruding on your sense of privacy? I asked myself.

"Throwing a party was the only thing I could come up with. Have a party and hope you'd come.

Losing your Aunt Victoria has been terribly hard on you. I just want to say to you, 'be happy, be well.'"

"I am well, Anthony. And, I'm okay, but I'm still sad. This party, well, it does feel too soon for me. Like I said, I came because of Tina. She's helped me through this time with such patience I felt she deserved a break from my mopey self."

"That's what I'm trying to point out, though, Sage. You won't let me in your life to help you through this time. I think *you* need a break from being mopey. But you won't come over for dinner, you don't say anything real on the phone. I did the only thing I could think of that might bring you out."

Anthony caught up Sage's hand. "Sage, all I want to say to you is that I *do* care deeply for you. Now, without your aunt hovering, instead of a stiff property-settlement proposal, I want to make a sincere, heart-felt proposal ...."

Sage pulled her hand away. "Oh, no!"

"I know, Sage, it's too soon. Please don't think I'm indiscreet, I'm just saying I've wanted to let you know that you're not alone in the world. I'm not interested in material things. Goodness knows I have lots of everything and I'm still lonely. Victoria couldn't imagine that there would or could ever be anyone but herself.

"To know you Sage is a rare gift in anyone's life. I'll drop this subject for the time-being. I just want to make sure that you're cared for, and not preyed upon."

A group of people wandered into the rose garden.

"Well," Anthony patted Sage's hand, "enough said. Now I can sleep peacefully because I let you know there *is* a safe haven. You're not entirely alone. Shall we re-join the party?"

"You go ahead, Anthony. I want to admire your roses and ... think for a while."

"As you wish, my dear. You look so pensive. Please be happy!" Anthony left the rose garden.

"You did great, Sage," she thought to herself. "You really let him know how you feel!"

She wished she could concentrate on the heady roses around her, but she found herself mentally wandering through the recent past, before Aunt Vicky was killed in the riding accident, when the three of them, she and Aunt Vicky and Anthony, would frequently go out together. How different this Anthony seemed from the serious, aloof man of those times. The warmest he'd ever been to her was perhaps to be paternal. Now he was affectionate. In addition, he seemed almost relieved, despite his sympathy, that Victoria was not around.

Sage reached into a more distant past, when she first came to stay with Aunt Vicky, after her parents had died. The worst time in her life. At that time Anthony was married. Strange that she hadn't thought of his wife in some time. Alison. Whatever happened to Alison? Such a nice, pretty woman, although quiet. That's what Sage particularly liked about her. She and Alison were both quiet and introverted.

There had been times, at parties not too different from this one, that Sage, an awkward, unhappy adolescent, and Alison, an unhappy, neglected wife, would sit on the sidelines, watching the activity swirl by, not saying much to each other, but enjoying one another's company all the same.

Well, Alison had fallen out of the picture somewhere along the line and all Aunt Vicky had to say about it was that Anthony had finally gotten rid of that excess baggage.

Sage's reverie was interrupted by the somewhat less than dulcet tones of Tina's voice nearby in the maze of the rose garden.

"She's in here somewhere, I know it!"

Sage stood. "If you're looking for me, here I am."

Tina popped up. "We saw Anthony wandering about alone and wondered where you were." She came around the corner with Michael and Millie in tow.

"Are you bored already?" Sage asked.

"Far, far from it. We were just talking about taking a tour around the mausoleum and I thought maybe you'd like to come along, although I know you're already familiar with the place."

"Sure, why not. Perhaps Michael knows the property better than I."

"I doubt it," Michael said in a reserved tone.

"Yeah. That brings up a question I have," Tina said. "If Sage has known Anthony for years, and you have probably always been his nephew, why don't you two know each other already?"

"Ah, well," Michael began, slightly ill-at-ease, "my family lives in Massachusetts. Uncle Anthony is actually my great-uncle, he's my grandfather's much younger brother. In fact, Anthony and my father are only a year apart. So, in the first place, my grandfather and he weren't close in age. Then, when Uncle Anthony came out here to be a rather, ahm, unorthodox business tycoon, the family lost track of him.

"I remember meeting him only once when I was a child," Michael went on. "He brought his wife, Alison, with him, I liked them both so much. I couldn't understand why everyone in the family always said his name in a whisper. I never heard from him until suddenly, I got a letter from him when I was an undergraduate at MIT, telling me he had an excellent job for me when I was 'through playing with school.'"

Michael studied the three feminine attentive faces and hitched his shoulders shyly. "I didn't come directly, but, to make a long and personal and boring story short, here I am."

"Not boring!" Tina said. "So that explains *that,* doesn't it, Sage?"

"I didn't ask!" Sage said, embarrassed.

"Oops, no you didn't. I'm the only nosey person here."

"I've wondered too," Millie piped up, "why you seem to like your uncle so much, but know almost nothing about him. I mean, I know things about him, 'cause, you know, he gets written up in in articles, and there's all the gossip about him at work. Of course that stuff is probably all a bunch of baloney, but ..." Millie trailed off. "Well, next intellectual discussion, I'll discuss physics, I promise."

Amused, Michael broke in, "let's take that tour and see if we can get lost in this place."

"Great idea, but with Sage, it's unlikely," Tina said. "She has an uncanny sense of location. I'm always telling her it's her Zuni blood, and she's always telling me it's her Zuni socialization."

"Oh, yes, you mentioned your mother was Zuni," Michael said.

Sage looked at Michael with new respect. "I'm impressed. People never seem to remember a tribe."

"I have a great and abiding respect for Native Americans," Michael said seriously. "I've made an effort to know a few things about as many tribes as I can, even though it's an endless study."

Michael had begun to lead Millie through the rose garden. Tina poked Sage in the ribs and raised an eyebrow, whispering, "beauty *and* brains!"

Sage smiled, but said nothing, trying to sort the onslaught of new information. Michael's comments touched her in a deep and secret place where almost no one had ever been, other than her darling mother.

"Come on," Tina urged, rushing to join Michael and Millie. "The Queen of Hearts has ordered the white roses painted red."

"Yes, yes, I'm coming," Sage answered. But I have nothing but heart's blood for the paint, she thought.

When the four of them came to the edge of the rose garden, the ocean, although several miles away, seemed to come to their feet. The plush night enveloped them and they fell silent.

"What's that phrase they say, when everyone becomes silent at the same moment, you know, that French or whatever ...." Millie asked.

"*Ange passe,*" Sage answered, "an angel passes."

"*Wow!*" Tina sighed.

Sage changed the subject. "Anthony owns all of the property downhill from here to the highway. Short of breaking our necks, this is all the further we can go. Toward the south he has grazing land and north are the ... the ..." she stuttered, "horse stables."

"Oh, yes," Michael said, "Uncle Anthony took me through them. He has some remarkable horse flesh it seems to me, although I don't know much about the creatures."

"I love horses," Millie said.

"Yes, he has some of the finest animals in the area," Sage said quietly. "Shall we go through the mansion?"

"Oh ..." Millie was disappointed. "Aren't we going to go look at the horses?"

"It's rough terrain between here and there."

"It's not a good idea, in the dark," Tina agreed.

"What a pity!" Millie pouted.

"Don't worry, Millie. I'll bring you over next week-end and we'll ride," Michael promised. "We'll all go."

"Well, okay, if it's a promise," Millie conceded.

"It's a promise. Will you join us, Tina and Sage?" Michael asked.

"I don't ... ride any more," Sage answered.

"And I never did ride," Tina added.

"Hmm. Well, all the more for us," Michael answered, sounding puzzled. "Let's go look at the house then."

"Castle," Millie corrected.

"Great idea," Tina agreed.

They skirted behind the orchestra. When they came to the mansion, Sage led them down several steps and through a side door virtually grown over with ivy.

"This is the wine cellar. We can access the small kitchen upstairs through here, and adjacent to that is the lounge."

They went upstairs and came out in the small kitchen, itself as big as an apartment.

They went into the adjoining room, the "lounge." Along one twenty-five foot wall was a full bar attended by three bartenders, more formally dressed than the people they waited on. On the opposite wall stood a massive stone-work fireplace. The room had dark mahogany walls and a mahogany beamed ceiling, furnished in mahogany furniture dimly lit with antique brass light fixtures, the upholstery and carpet a deep burgundy. A wonderful essence of exotic spices wove through the air.

"What a wonderful aroma," Michael said.

"Mulled wine," Sage waved at a huge cauldron, steam rising from it. "It's one of Anthony's specialties. It's truly wonderful. It's curious how it puts you in exactly the mood you'd like to be in. If you're sad and you wish you were happy, it cheers you up. If you feel fidgety and you wish you'd settle down, it calms you ...."

"A magic elixir," Michael said.

"Exactly!"

"Well, then, what are we waiting for?" Tina led the way to the cauldron. A sober middle-aged woman poured four cut-crystal cups of the heady-smelling potion.

"What now?" Tina asked.

"My favorite room is the library," Sage answered.

"*Ish!*" Tina and Millie said together, while at the same moment Michael said, "perfect!"

"Divided opinion again!" Tina said.

"No, no, the library is fine," Millie amended. "I know Michael loves books!"

They passed from the lounge into a long mahogany hall, busts in little niches along the walls, delicate lighting warming the wood tones, thick, cushioned carpet underfoot. They passed three or four busts when Michael stopped.

"Einstein?" He backed up to the previous one. "Bach?"

"I'd have thought you had gone down this hall," Sage said.

"No. All I've been in is the front entry, the dining room, some study, and the bedroom I stayed in. And, oh yes, I guess it's the 'big' kitchen."

"You'll see he has no busts of family," Sage said. "I believe I'm quoting Anthony fairly accurately when I say that he says the only family he claims is the family of great minds. I'm sure there's no offense meant, by the way, Michael."

"Oh no! Who am I to be offended? I agree with him."

At the end of the hall Sage pushed at a point on the mahogany paneling, and an invisible door slid open. They stepped through the doorway.

Tina, Millie and Michael openly and silently gawked at the library before them. A three-story, forty-by-thirty foot room, with thousands and thousands of books on the walls, little wrought iron stairways running up the walls, wrought iron cat-walks on the walls around the room, deep cavernous green velvet, over-stuffed furniture scattered about like flotsam, floor and table lamps with beaded shades, and potted palms everywhere like jetsam, giant tables with giant atlases spread out on them, and a mahogany parquet floor with dense red and green oriental carpets.

The door they came through, closed behind them, invisibly, silently.

They moved quietly into the room. To their left was a cozy and crackling fire. Over the mantle hung a life-sized canvas of a beautiful, but aloof-looking woman, astride a black, fine-boned, high-strung, Arabian horse. Standing by the horse, her hand reaching up to pet the horse's mane, but looking out pensively across the library was a stunning, huge-eyed girl, her blonde, animate, hair caught forever, buoyed up in a breeze.

"Oh! Sage!" Tina said reverently, eyes transfixed.

"My, my," Michael whispered.

"I can't believe he put it *here*, when he knows how I love this room," Sage sounded distressed, and turned her back on the painting.

"But ... it's *beautiful*," Millie whispered.

"It used to belong to my Aunt Victoria. I sent it to Anthony a couple weeks ago."

Sage moved across the room and sat with her back to the painting, sipping her wine.

"Well, I don't understand," Millie said.

In hushed tones, Tina told Michael and Millie that only a few weeks before, the beautiful woman in the painting, Sage's aunt Victoria, had been thrown from that very horse and died.

The three of them came over to Sage, pulling chairs close to her.

"I'm sorry, Sage," Michael said. "We're clods."

Sage looked up from her wine, tears in her eyes. "No, you didn't know. But Anthony does, that's what surprises me. Anthony had it commissioned as a present for her when I was thirteen. I was still in deep mourning over my parents death. I've never liked it because of that. Aunt Vicky, however, was exceptionally fond of it, and hung it over the fireplace in her private rooms. But since the accident, I really couldn't stand it. I gave it back to him. I don't understand why he would hang it in my favorite room ...."

Michael reached over and patted her shoulder. "I'm sure he didn't mean to hurt you. Let's try sipping our mood-changing wine for the time-being."

At that moment a great door opposite the fireplace slid open and Anthony entered.

"I guess I know where you can be found," he said, smiling at Sage. He took in the painting on the wall behind them. "Oh, no Sage. I'm sorry! That painting ... I expressly told Robert to make sure it came down before tonight. What an over-sight! I'll have a word or two with Robert."

"Please, no, Anthony. It doesn't matter," Sage rose in dismay. "He has so much to take care of and worry about, without trying to remember to take down a painting. You see, I just sit with my back to it, chatting with my wonderful friends."

"I apologize again, Sage, But it's such a stunning rendering of you …." Anthony paused.

"It's all right, Anthony, really. We're sitting here, sipping the wonderful mulled wine, taking in the ambience …."

"Yes, yes," they all chorused, "we're having a lovely time."

"Good! Well, you can come back later, but right now, I've got the orchestra all ready to do a set of Strauss waltzes. I need you, Sage, to show these neophytes how it's done."

"Waltz? Of course!" Sage rose, clearly happy. "Come on everyone, I love to waltz!"

"Not me," Michael protested.

"Why not?" Sage asked.

"I've never waltzed."

"That's not an excuse that holds up around here," Sage said. "Tina is an excellent teacher. What about you, Millie?"

"No, my experience is pretty much disco-limited."

"Fine," Anthony said happily. "Two new waltz recruits!" He grabbed Sage's hand and hurried her toward the door.

"Anthony loves a waltz and won't take no for an answer," Sage called over her shoulder.

Michael, Millie, and Tina looked at one another. Tina stood. "Come on … when in Rome! … You won't know until you've tried."

On the dance floor constructed for the party, Michael, Millie, Tina, and everyone else, stood around the dance floor watching Anthony and Sage swirl around and around to "The Blue Danube."

"How pretty they are!" Sage heard Millie say to Michael as she and Anthony whirled by. "They look like they ought to be on top of a music box!"

When the music stopped, everyone applauded. Anthony beamed.

"Thank you, everyone, for coming to my party. I also want to thank my partner, Sage Elgin, for coming tonight at my special request. As some of you know, she has recently had great misfortune in her life, and I want her to know how much she honors me by coming to my home. I've given this party expressly for her, to let her know she has friends who love and cherish her."

Mortified, Sage hoped to shrink under the parquet flooring while everyone applauded and cheered. Looking around, she saw her neighbors, and business men with their wives, and Tina and Michael, and even Millie, a new acquaintance, and saw real sympathy and true caring in their faces.

She saw Tina wipe away a tear. Sage put her self-consciousness on hold to silently give thanks to all the blessings her life held, to the people who cared about her. She felt herself pull out of that dark place she'd been in for the last two months.

Anthony put a protective arm around Sage's shoulders, then said, "Now, everybody waltz! I need a man to initiate Millie Watson into ballroom dancing."

Sage saw Millie cringe, but she grinned when she was instantly flocked with half-a-dozen men and swept onto the dance floor.

Then Tina took Michael's hand and pulled him onto the floor.

Hours later, after many pairs of shoes had been kicked off by the dancers, Sage sank into a chair by the side of the dance floor, then noticed that she'd sat next to Michael, who sat with his back to the dance floor, eyes closed, tapping out the rhythm of the music on a wine glass.

"Are you a waltz convert yet?" she asked.

Michael opened his eyes and sat up.

"Convert is a strong word. Appreciator is more accurate."

"Millie seems to be enjoying herself. Have you danced with her at all tonight?"

"Nope. Couldn't get next to her. Well, this is a big night for her. I'm glad it turned out so well. I suppose I'll have to listen to her talk about this party every day for weeks, but it's nice to see her happy. She comes from a pretty meager background."

"Umm." They're together every day, Sage thought, they must live together. "How was Tina, as a teacher?"

"Great, she's truly great. I think I can at least fake a waltz. Uncle Anthony is right, it *is* fun. I mercifully let Tina go, we kept getting cut in on."

Sage looked over the dance floor for her friend, finally spotted her, eyes glowing, dancing with an attractive man whose face, but not his name, was familiar to Sage. She didn't see Millie at all. She spotted Anthony dancing with the dowager princess.

"A pretty good party," Michael said, leaning back in his chair, closing his eyes again.

"Yes," Sage agreed, taking a surreptitious glance at the lovely plane of Michael's cheekbone, his strong yet boyish mouth, wondering how Millie could spend even a minute away from him. "A lovely party."

Chapter 7
Michael

Michael lived in a two story, two bedroom plus den, two-and-a-half bath condo in Irvine. A nice enough place. At least he finally lived alone, was close to work, and had a two stall garage to work on his vintage cars. He told himself that his life was everything a man could hope for. Women clearly found him attractive, he had an excellent job, and he had a nice place to live.

Then why, he wondered, this particular Sunday evening, did he feel so hollow, so aimless, so lonely? Not exactly unhappy, but definitely not happy. Empty. He'd spent his entire life learning things he could put to practical use. But of what use was practical use if he lived his life alone, if he couldn't find someone who had goals of her own, and who wanted to share similar goals with someone in her life?

He hated it when people said people were "types," but his experience lately seemed to fall into two "types" of women. One was the ambitious, focused, career-oriented woman, which was fine, but why did they seem so cold? There was one such woman in his immediate work environment. Because of his natural shyness, he rarely spoke to her.

One Friday in February he wished her a happy Valentine's Day. She growled that it wasn't Valentine's Day. He felt it unnecessary to point out that Valentine's Day was the next day, a Saturday. The following week he received a memo that he'd been written up for "inappropriate innuendo" because of this exchange.

The other type of woman went over-board the other direction. They didn't care what they did or could do, they just talked about getting married, and how giving themselves up completely to a man to make him happy would make them happy. He wanted to ask them how could this phantom man be happy if there was nothing to talk about between them?

Well, and then there were the playgirls, but they didn't even make it to his list.

He reassured himself there was another kind of woman. His ideal woman. He just hadn't met her yet.

Unbidden, Sage came into his mind. Which type was she? Probably the second type, on the road to making his Uncle Anthony happy. Although clearly intelligent and interesting, would she allow her intelligence and her interests to take second place to making his uncle happy.

Michael went into the garage and surveyed the disemboweled carburetor of the MGA. It needed another rebuild kit, something had been wrong with one of the gaskets of the previous rebuild kit. He couldn't do anything on the MGA until the kit came.

The Audi, "old reliable," didn't need any work done on it.

He went back into the house, into his den-made-library and picked up the most recent book he'd gotten on gold-mining and gold-panning.

Settling into his comfortable, dark-grey wing-backed chair, he propped his feet up on the hassock and began reading. The chapter was about the gold discovered in Scotland, interesting enough, but after a few minutes he found his mind wandering.

Maybe, he thought, he should quit his job. Drop everything and go to Scotland, become a bearded hunter of gold and never be heard from again. Some part of him wanted that more than anything. It wasn't that he desired to become rich. He came from a wealthy family who would support him if he did nothing, and he had both skill and talent enough as a computer chip designer to make excellent money.

Gold-panning was hard work, it took skill, knowledge, and intuition. But he loved the experience for the freedom of living in nature.

He put the book down and stalked about his study. He needed to *do* something. He thought of Millie. Maybe she'd play some racquetball. She was a good partner, she kept him on his toes.

Millie answered the phone in an un-Millie-like quiet voice.

"What's the matter with you? Are you sick?"

"Heartsick," Millie answered.

"On, no, not another sob story! Millie, when are you going to learn how to get these guys to treat you right?"

"It's easy for you to say, Michael, but you just don't understand what it is to be a plain woman ... you're a beautiful man, the world was made for you."

"Oh please, Millie, you're cute and personable. We've had this discussion before."

"I know."

"Right now I want to do something, I don't want to think, I just want to work out some aggressions."

"Ah, burgeoning testosterone," Millie said.

"I thought you might want to play some racquetball."

"It sounds great, if you don't mind that I'm in a man-hating mood."

"You won't remember it after fifteen minutes on the court. Clean out all the poisons and you'll feel like a winner ... even when I beat you."

"*Hah!* We'll see about that. Woodbridge Courts?"

"Yeah," Michael said, unbuttoning his shirt, feeling better already. "Meet you there."

On the racquetball court Michael rooted Millie on, "Yeah, Millie, that's it, give it to him, whoever he is."

"I am!" she answered, whacking the ball. "That so-and-so!"

Michael lost the ball, laughing. "That so-and-so? Do people actually *say* that?"

"I didn't want to use strong language in front of a gentleman. You can be sure I've called him worse in the last few days."

"Hit this ball some more. You're still angry."

They battled out another game, gave up the notion of keeping score and just took out their frustrations on the ball.

"Okay," Michael said, "that's enough of this stuff. I think I've gotten the exercise I needed."

"And I even worked out some of my man-hating," Millie agreed. "Although not all. I really do feel better. It's surprising."

"No it's not. Fresh oxygen in your blood pumping into your head will make you feel better every time. Clears out the cobwebs."

"Hmm. Cobwebs. I may not be super bright, but I'm not so slow that spiders make nests in my head."

"Of course not. Let's go get some pizza."

"Yeah. Pizza sounds great."

In the dark interior of the rowdy pizza parlor, Michael sat across from Millie and studied her. Her color was high, making her look particularly charming. But, still, a cast of worry or sadness—or both—lingered in her eyes.

"Okay pal, friend of mine, tell me the story," Michael said.

"Aww ...."

"I'm sorry! It was out of your mind, wasn't it? And I reminded you."

"No, not really. But why should I bring us both down?"

"My idea is to bring you up!"

"The only way you could make me utterly and unbelievably happy is not in the cards. You're way out of my league, you made that perfectly clear to me with your interest in that incredible beauty with the strange name."

"I guess you mean Sage."

"I guess I do. I guess you do too."

"We're supposed to be talking about you, Millie!"

"Me. I'm so boring. *Sooo* boring. No wonder nobody loves me, cherishes me. I know, you care about me, but ...."

"Why are you so awful about yourself?"

"I'd love to be able to say I'm gorgeous and wonderful and a really good catch. But facts is facts. I'm not. And so, I get toyed with. Do you remember the man I was dancing with at Anthony's party?"

"Which one?! You were swamped."

"However it may have seemed to you, I began with this guy and ended up with this guy. I thought he was wonderful. Of course, I'm not used to men doting on me the way he did."

"Michael, your pizza is ready," an intercom blared.

"Hold that thought, Millie," Michael stood. "I'll be right back." He soon returned carrying a gigantic pizza, warm bread aroma enveloping them in their cozy booth. "Sustenance!" Without ceremony, Michael hefted giant slices of pizza onto a couple plates. "Continue—so you're not used to men behaving like this still nameless man ...."

"Bill. Bill-the-louse. Yeah. He's attractive, but in a sort-of untrustworthy way. You say to yourself, is this guy actually slimy, or are his eyes just deep-set and he can't help that? Turns out, both points are true. He's Sage's attorney and he was only friendly to me because he saw me hanging around with her. He thought I was a personal friend of hers."

"He *said* that?"

"Pretty much. After he'd taken me out to dinner a couple times he started in on me about when I was going to see her, and I said I didn't know. After a couple of other ... ahm, social events, he continued nagging me about her. I finally told him I hardly knew her. Then he got mean, and quite frankly, really weird." Millie shuddered. "He never even called me after that."

Michael shook his head, consternation furrowing his brow. Something troubled him deeply, something beyond even what Millie had just shared. "This gives me a bad feeling. A really bad feeling. Clearly the best part of your story is the fact that you got rid of him."

Millie nodded, while sadness continued to cloud her pixie features. "I know you're right. But I got so involved so fast. He *doted* on me. Or so it seemed. And then to realize that everything he said and everything he did was simply flat-out lies—how can anyone be so *entirely* deceitful? How can a person live with themselves, knowing they've hurt someone else like that?"

"I imagine, my dear little Millie, he has no clue that he's hurt you. He sounds sociopathic. The type of person incapable of empathy—good at getting people to do what he wants, but cannot even grasp the notion that those people have thoughts, feelings, and desires of their own."

"It's as if you really know him, Michael. Well, he just ought to be struck mute so he can't do that anymore, that's what I think."

"Sounds like the perfect punishment. I can't shake how dark the mental image of this guy is to me. I wonder why Sage has such a questionable character for an attorney?"

"Yeah. I wondered too. She seems nice and honest, so why would she employ someone really shifty? And she's smart, wouldn't she know he's a crook? Maybe I'm not being fair. Maybe he's okay as an attorney, but lousy in a relationship. But my instincts say, 'this guy is trouble.'"

"I'm going with your instincts." Michael leaned back. "When it comes to women's instincts, I stand in awe. You know you're better off without him, Millie, so cut your losses, take your heart back, and move on."

"If only my instincts would kick in sooner! Except for with you Michael. The moment I laid eyes on you I knew you were good-hearted. I've never been wrong about that. Like today, I needed someone to talk with, to help me get back in focus, *so much*. And here you are! You called me up, made me exercise, and now, you're feeding me."

"That's what friends are for, my little pizza eater," Michael said, patting her hand.

Chapter 8
Sage

Sage thrashed through Aunt Victoria's massive walnut desk, trying to sort out the paperwork she'd need for the impeding appointment with Bill Rattnor, wondering which part of the chore she hated more—finding out how much *more* deeply in debt Aunt Vicky's estate was in, or having to be alone with Bill Rattnor, whom she viscerally disliked. And, she knew, that feeling was mutual.

"What *is* your bookkeeping system, Aunt Vicky? Oriental carpets under 'P,' along with alcohol, cars and horses." She found a cover sheet in the middle of the file. All that was on it were the words: "Miscellaneous Pleasures."

"Ah! I get it, 'P' is for pleasure." She stuffed the documents regarding carpets, alcohol, cars and horses under the cover sheet and returned the file to its place. Just then, the front door chimes reverberated through the house.

"*Ish!* There he is." She stepped into a pair of heels, then let Bill in and led him to Victoria's office. She had the fleeting thought that one did not invite the vampire into one's home.

"How are you, Sage?" he asked in a sinuous, too-familiar voice as they walked down the hall.

She could feel his dark eyes on her while she moved to sit behind the desk. "Please, Mr. Rattnor, have a seat. I've been well, thank you."

"That's good." He continued to stare at her. "You were fairly out of sorts."

Sage closed her eyes and gathered herself. Everything that came out of this man's mouth and his whole entire *presence* crawled under her skin and laid little eggs of revulsion.

"Out of sorts, Mr. Rattnor? I didn't have the flu ...."

"Sorry," he said, sounding more insincere than ever, "I always seem to express myself poorly when I'm around you. You're such a stickler for words. Your Aunt Victoria never seemed to care what I said, as long as I did my job."

You don't like me, I don't like you, Sage thought. So let's get on with business and get this over with. She slid open the desk drawer and pulled out the file she'd compiled. "I've been going through files." She noted him shift uneasily out of the corner of her eye.

As she thumbed through the paper work, she continued, "and, although Aunt Victoria had an unorthodox method of filing, I've gotten the gist of it. What I'm getting at is, there are several things I cannot find any trace of at all. For example," she turned her attention back to Rattnor, matching him stare for stare. "I can't find a single trace of the Petrol-Fill papers. Not anything."

Bill shrank ever so slightly from her gaze. Maybe, she thought, I can get the upper hand with this snake.

But the snake quickly hooded his eyes, and stared her down. "Don't worry your pretty blonde tresses about such things," he all but hissed. "Why would you bother with this stuff? You've got better things to do. Places to go, things to see, men to go out with."

Sage's ire rose. "Mr. Rattnor, let's make some things extremely clear. First of all, your are not to discuss my personal life. Secondly, I concern myself with issues that are, indeed, my business, whether you approve or not. And thirdly, I can't spend time or money going places, doing things, when I daily receive information about how all the businesses in my aunt's estate are hemorrhaging money. Money that I cannot trace. It's your job to fully apprise me, the executor of her will, of any operation I choose to investigate."

She lowered her voice to clarify her resolve. "If you cannot do what you are paid to do, you will be replaced."

Bill Rattnor stood, braced his knuckles on the edge of the desk and leaned toward Sage. There was something like a smile pasted across his mouth, but his eyes were cold, flat steel. "Little girl, I have no time to teach you, simply because you have whims, how to understand your aunt's business. I've plenty enough to do trying to salvage what I can from her frivolous and selfish life style ....”

With that, Sage rose as well, and, in her heels, dominated him. She stood straight, arms at her sides, her anger a deadly calm. “Mr. Rattnor, you are never, under any circumstance, to refer to my Aunt in any remotely negative terms within my hearing. Victoria’s life-style was her business. Additionally, I am not, by any stretch of the definition, a ‘little girl.’

“You will not patronize me. You will treat me with respect. You will perform your services as I see fit.” She folded her arms, half a gnat’s breath from firing him. “You have one of two courses of action. You can sit, and we’ll continue this appointment, or you can find your own way to the door for the last and final time.”

Bill Rattnor picked up his briefcase and left. Sage listened to the angry click of his heels across the foyer marble, winced when the heavy door slammed.

She stood, unmoving for a few moments, still believing he’d return. But he didn’t, and she slowly sank into the chair. What had just happened? She felt she’d won some kind of psychic battle, but feared she’d begun a war.

Why would there be a war? What was Rattnor’s problem? Could it be that spending time with her clarifying the books really angered him? Although Aunt Victoria’s accounts and business were extensive, he was on exclusive contract with her, which made him now exclusively Sage’s attorney. She was his boss. He was her employee. Why did he appear to not understand that?

She returned to the files, vexed and confused. What to do now? The overwhelming muddle of her Aunt's filing just about did her in.

Half-an-hour later the phone rang. It was Bill's secretary. "One moment please, Miss Elgin, Mr. Rattnor wishes to speak with you."

Bill came on the line. "Sage! Glad you're still there," his said in his saccharin, metallic voice. "Are you calmed down now?"

"*Me?!*" Sage asked, amazed.

"Now don't get excited again. I just wanted to call and unruffle your feathers. You want to look at the Petrol-Fill files. Of course, I have them, in a safe. I'll come over Friday to go over them with you."

"How about right now?" Sage answered.

"Sage, you forfeited your appointment time with me today by suggesting I leave. You have a life of leisure. I have a life of work. I'm booked until Friday."

"Mr. Rattnor, I don't need you present in order to look at *my* files. I'll be over directly to look at them myself."

"As I said, they are in a safe, Sage. The whole world isn't set up just for your whimsy."

"Make copies, have them delivered. I'll expect them no later than tomorrow afternoon."

Sage hung up. Bill Rattnor really hated her, deeply. And in some sense that she couldn't understand, he hated her beyond herself. She didn't know *what* the hate was, or *why* it was, but it left her quivering even after she walked out of Aunt Victoria's office in an effort to get away from his horrible steel-cold presence.

*   *

However, Sage was surprised when a package containing copies of the Petrol-Fill files was delivered the next morning. She took the package into the kitchen, brewed some tea, then began to spread out the files' contents on the kitchen counter.

They were in terrible chronological disarray. Receipts and notes from different times had been photo-copied together on the same sheets of paper, some documents had been reduced so much they were nearly impossible to read. She got out scissors and cut apart the unrelated documents, continuing to put them in chronological order.

She put everything into the best order she could, made some fresh tea and began to study the documents in earnest. The more she looked, the more holes she saw. There was every indication that Petrol-Fill functioned in the green, but the bottom-line numbers were frighteningly in the red. A chill ran through her as an unavoidable conclusion rose.

She must be wrong!

She moved away from the strewn papers to clear her head, reminding herself that she had no background in business. She probably didn't understand what she was looking at. On the other hand, she was not stupid. Something was profoundly amiss with the Petrol-fill files. In addition to hating her, Sage realized that Bill Rattnor must think she was a blithering idiot.

She meandered out to the flower garden, pacing over the neglected black crushed-rock paths, deep in thought. Leaves and debris overtook the walks, the flowers had grown wild and unchecked, or were on dead stalks, or were choked with ivy. The hedges had fallen into complete disarray, like school boys without hair cuts.

Poor neglected garden, Sage thought, sitting on an ornate Victorian black wrought iron bench. It had been such a show place, and now it's a ... hide place. She sipped her tea and looked around at the bleak unhappy garden, thinking about the Petrol-Fill files, thinking about the garden.

She stood up and strode into the house. Twenty minutes later, dressed in jeans, an old shirt, work boots and gloves, she carried garden tools into the flower garden. She would capture two birds with one chore—work on the garden and think about the Petrol-Fill files—and improve both.

She pruned and clipped and watered and raked and cleared until mid-afternoon. Then she gathered the garden tools, dragged the six trash bags she'd filled to the trash and put the tools away, feeling invigorated. A garden was a good thing to tend!

She took a long hot bath, pulled on her favorite peach-colored silk outfit and began again to look at the papers strewn over the kitchen counters. It had come to her, as she worked in the flower garden, that the largest incongruities were near her Aunt's death.

Her study confirmed it.

What should she do now? Hire another attorney? Who? Who could she trust? Who could walk into this mess and make sense of it? Peeved, then angry, she circled the kitchen. A niggling thought that perhaps she ought to be a bit frightened rose up. Bill Rattnor—with his peculiar dark personality—how far would he go to protect what appeared to even Sage's untrained eye to be a brazen embezzlement?

"What are friends for?" she finally said, resigned. Picking up the phone, she called Anthony, relieved when he, himself, answered.

"I really hate to bother you, Anthony, but ...."

"Good grief, Sage, you're never a bother. I couldn't be happier hearing your voice."

"Thank you, Anthony. But ... this is actually a business call. I need your opinion on a file Bill Rattnor sent over this morning at my insistence. I'd bring it to you, but I've got it strewn all over my kitchen counters in discrete piles and ...."

"No problem, Sage."

Sage heard a burst of giggles in the background. "Oh! You have company ...."

"Michael and Millie have been out riding. They just came in and are acting fresh-air goofy." Sage could hear the affection in Anthony's voice.

She chuckled, happy to hear a nuance of joy in Anthony's voice that she'd never heard. "Okay, you 'kids' all enjoy yourselves. This boring paperwork can wait."

"Nonsense. Those kids can take care of themselves. I'll be over in about an hour, if that suits you."

"If you're sure ... wait, I have an idea. Bring Michael and Millie with you. They can play in the garden while you and I look at the papers for a bit ... you'll probably look a this muddle for five minutes and have it—and me—all straightened out. I'll make my famous spaghetti dinner."

"Oh! I didn't know your spaghetti dinners were famous."

"I misled you—it's the person on the jars of spaghetti sauce in my pantry who is famous. But I can and will make a gigantic salad from scratch."

Anthony laughed. "It sounds wonderful. A casual dinner with my favorite people. I'll bring bread and wine."

Sage hung up, then looked around the paper-strewn kitchen. What was she thinking? She never even cooked for *herself*, and now, with the kitchen in complete mayhem, she'd invited three people over. One of whom made her pulse race. The image of Michael's profile the night he drove her to her door in the darkened limo came back to her, as if etched on her very synapses. The look of him—not just that he was so attractive—but something else, as if she'd been with him before, a discomforting feeling that she needed to be near him.

He's not available, she reminded herself. Sighing deeply, she turned her back to the muddle of paperwork, leaned against the counter and rubbed her forehead, willing all the jangling thoughts to be still.

At that moment, the front door chimes rang. Sage glanced up at the clock. Surely it wasn't Anthony already? She wandered to the front door, hoping it wasn't Anthony just yet, also hoping it wasn't some annoying salesperson, when she saw Bill Rattnor though the beveled glass of the door, pacing back and forth. Tempted to step back and avoid him altogether, it was too late. He saw her and stood facing her at the door.

She opened the door a crack. "I'm sorry, Mr. Rattnor, I don't have time to talk with you right now."

"Oh yes you do," he said, pushing his way into the foyer.

Shocked, Sage backed away from him. "Please leave. I'm requesting politely, but I'm serious."

"I am so fed up with you," he said through gritted teeth. *"I am so fed up with you!* You've been a pain from the first day you entered this house until this moment. I'm going to try and talk some sense into you, but I'm warning you, I'm at the end of my tether."

Sage took another step back, fear running ice water through her. "Mr. Rattnor, for the last time, leave my home. Furthermore, you are no longer in my employ. I nearly fired you yesterday. Now add breaking and entering, and threatening me, and we have reached the termination of your involvement with my aunt's estate and with me."

She moved cautiously around him and opened the door wide. "And we will see what falls out regarding your probable embezzlement." As soon as she said this, Sage regretted it. Not wise to poke a stick at the tiger, she thought to herself.

And she was right. She could hardly believe the transformation that appeared before her. Rattnor's eyes became slivers, his teeth crunched together roping his jaw, his face flushed a fire-anger red, and his entire body became ramrod, every muscle clinched.

"Shut up," he hissed. "shut up, shut up, *shut up!* I have *had* it with you Elgin bitches. First one then the other. Flaunting your bodies around, teasing. Flaunting your money. You don't deserve one single cent. You ought to be living in a tent. Who are you? Nobody, *nothing.* You've never done anything worthwhile in your life. Never lifted a finger.

"I've slaved around the clock, day in and day out. And for what? Only to have you think you can tell me I'm fired? Well, that's not going to happen, little girl. What's going to happen is another accident. Perfect too. Just like your Aunt. Perfect justice. You miss her so much? We'll just have you join her."

He reached out to grab her, she stepped back behind the door. "What are you saying? What are you saying about Victoria?"

A rictus grin crossed his features. "Nothing. Just that, it looked like her horse threw her. Her horse, that she loved more than anything or anyone. That she'd raised from birth. And excellent rider that she was, too."

Rattnor grabbed her, trapped behind the door. With lightning strength, he spun her around and pinned her arms behind her back. "And you're going to have an accident too."

In a steel grip that stunned her, that she could not escape, he dragged her backwards across the foyer. "I can just see the headlines now, 'beautiful heiress tumbles down her own winding stairway.' So sad, too bad. Cut short in the midst of her frivolities."

They reached the bottom of the stairs. "*Let. Me. Go!*" Sage screamed in his ear, struggling with every bit of her strength.

"*Shut up!*" He slapped her across the face so hard she became disoriented.

He dragged her up three steps. "Have to get high enough to accomplish the goal."

"Think about what you're doing," she tried to reason.

"I have thought about this long and hard, for many hours, you can count on it. Shut up." He dragged her up another couple of steps.

"Anthony is on his way over," she whispered, knowing that, if Rattnor was successful, Anthony would be too late.

Rattnor stopped and looked down at her incredulously. "Oh, that's pathetic! You must think I'm utterly stupid. Honestly, Victoria, I am so sick of the way you patronize me. I'm so sick of you thinking you're superior to me."

"Sage," Sage said.

"What?"

"You said Victoria. Victoria is dead. Apparently you killed her. I'm Sage."

He looked confused for a brief moment then shook his head. "Who cares? There's no difference between the two of you. One of you, two of you, ten of you, it's all the same. You're this endless monster in my life. Soon to be over. What I've worked on so long and hard will finally be mine. Finally!" He dragged her up another step.

"How so?"

"Don't you remember willing everything to me in that giant stack of papers I had you sign in our executor meeting. You don't? Never mind, it's all taken care of. Not to worry."

Sage kicked off her heels and got some traction on the carpet. "If I'm going down, you crazy creep, you're going with me." She gambled on the six or seven steps being a less dangerous fall that the entire stairway.

Throwing everything into her thrust, she lurched on top of him, and they rolled to the bottom of the stairs.

As Sage felt herself slip into unconsciousness, she heard car doors slamming and, at some distance it seemed, yelling.

But it just didn't seem to matter to pay any attention to it. She saw Aunt Victoria far away, in a glorious light-filled meadow of sunflowers. It seemed like the perfect place to be.

Chapter 9
Sage's Friends

Sage regained consciousness slowly, drowsy and confused. She opened her eyes. She wondered where she was ... she didn't recognize the room at first and then her eyes found the little oval antique picture of the Cupid she was fond of. She finally realized she was in her own room, with the breeze blowing through the pale green ruffled glass curtains at the window.

Very strange how unfamiliar it appeared at first. She tried to understand why she felt so foggy.

"Oh, wonderful! You've come to," a woman said behind her.

Sage turned to see who was talking to her. A blinding flash of pain shot through her shoulder. *"Ohhh!"* She winced as she made out Millie.

Millie scooted the little boudoir chair near Sage. "Sorry. I didn't mean to startle you. What hurts?"

"My shoulder. In fact, both of my shoulders. *Ohh!*"

It came back to her ... Rattnor dragging her backwards by her pinned arms across the floor and up the stairs. "*Oh!*" She started to shiver involuntarily.

"There, there, now, everything is going to be all right." Millie leapt up from the chair. "Let me get Anthony. He's talking to the police. They ... they took that crazy scumbag away."

"No, stay, Millie. If Anthony's ... let him finish that business. You, please, stay with me."

"Okay," Millie came back to the little chair, then reached out and patted Sage's hand. "Poor Sage. What a monster he is. I shudder to think ... that is ... I'm so glad we came early. Anthony wanted to come right away after you called. He was really ... it's almost as if he knew. He practically shoved us into the car. I wanted to change but he said, 'no, bring your stuff and change at Sage's.' And he was right, wasn't he?"

"He was," Sage agreed, starting to nod, then thinking better of it. She sighed deeply, "Oh, that hurts too."

"The doctor said you are pretty bruised, but no broken bones."

"Oh! My doctor was here? How long have I been out?"

"I believe it's Anthony's private physician. He came right away. He was here before the police even. Then the police came and Michael carried you up here while Anthony talked to them. The doctor had me stay here to watch you."

"Thank you," Sage said simply. "You're so sweet."

"Oh, well, no, I'm not. Anyway, it's enough to know that that horrible person will be put away." There were tears in Millie's eyes. "He'll be put away where he can't hurt anyone, anymore!"

There was a knock at the door.

"Come in," Sage called.

Anthony opened the door. He and Michael stood at the door.

"Well, come on in you two." She started to wave them in, and stopped, wincing at the pain. "I can't seem to get it through my head that my shoulders hurt."

Despite it all, however, Sage smiled, a feeling of gratitude welling up inside her that was larger than she could express in words.

These three people had saved her life. Michael, again! She felt tears escape.

"Are you all right?" Anthony came to the other side of the bed.

Sage patted the bed for him to sit. "I'm ... it's just, I'm so grateful. I'm so fortunate."

"Fortunate? Dear girl, you've just been beaten and have fallen down a flight of stairs."

"But you all saved my life. I am *so grateful*. Thank you." She looked at each of them in turn, and even Michael, who still stood in the doorway, had tears in his eyes. "Come in Michael. Don't stand out there in the cold," Sage continued, "come in to the warmth of the family." She gestured to the love seat by the window.

Michael crossed the room to the love seat. Everyone was silent, watching him. He looked around at them all, then said, "For my next act ...."

Sage and Millie giggled.

"I think we could all use some tea," Millie said.

"Oh, yes, please," Sage agreed. "Sorry about all the paperwork on the counters in the kitchen."

"No problem. Anthony mentioned on the way over that that's why he was coming in the first place, to help you sort that out. I'll work around it."

The front door chimes rang through the house. "And I'll get that on my way."

The three of them listened as Millie opened the door. She called up the stairs, "Anthony, it's a detective. He wants to ask some more questions."

Anthony patted Sage's hand. "I'll be right back."

There was a moment of awkward silence between Sage and Michael.

"How have you been?" Sage finally asked.

"Fine. Keeping busy." Michael's tone was cool.

"Are you ... angry with me?" Sage asked, puzzled.

"No. No, I'm not angry with you. I'm just, I guess I'm confused."

"Confused by what?" Sage breathed deeply, willing the pain and fog in her head to stop so she could clearly understand Michael.

"I don't understand how you could have this Bill Rattnor anywhere around you in your life ...."

"Oh. Well. You're right. Absolutely right. It's fallout from my being too nice. Why didn't I fire him before? I almost did, yesterday. And why didn't Aunt Victoria fire him? I don't know the answer to that question. Why I didn't fire him—I didn't want to hurt him. I didn't like him. I didn't trust him. But ... I was, simply, too nice."

Michael nodded, still unconvinced. "He's a bad person."

"I know," Sage agreed. "I have the bruises to testify."

"Yes. You do. You're going to have that shiner for a while."

"Shiner?"

"Black eye. Bruised face."

Sage brought her hand to her face, wincing at the pain in her shoulder. "Oh!" She exclaimed, touching her cheek. "Now, that's sore. I must be quite a sight." She waved at the little mirror on her dresser. "Can you hand me that?"

Michael hesitated. "No. I don't think I should."

"That bad?" She started to stand, cried out in pain and slumped back on the bed.

"Okay, all right. Ill hand you the mirror." He came over to the bedside with the mirror.

"Sit," Sage ordered, making him take the chair Millie vacated. She held the mirror up to her face and gasped. "Oh! Who is that? Wow. Swollen, black and blue." She closed her eyes and breathed deeply.

"Are you okay?" Michael's voiced was edged with worry.

"Not really. I'll be okay. Ya shoulda seen the other guy! Ha!" Sage leaned back into the pillows. "Yeah, I'm pretty sore."

"The doctor gave you some sort of injection and left pain meds."

"Good to know. By the way, thanks for carrying me up here. Sorry for the almost dead weight."

"You have a dark side, don't you?"

"I suspect it's temporary. A coping mechanism. But let's get back to why you seem to be angry with me?"

"Not angry. I'm mystified. Women can be … mystifying."

"True. Where are you headed with this?"

"Apparently Bill Rattnor acted as though he was interested in Millie, and it seems Millie fell for him—and his line. But he was only trying to get close to her because he thought she was a personal friend of yours. I don't know why he couldn't go to you directly, but …."

"Excuse me Michael, for a moment. I'm a little confused … aren't you and Millie, ah, a couple?"

"Millie and me? In a relationship? No. We're good friends, but, no. Why would you think ….?"

"At Anthony's party you'd said something about seeing each other every day. That seemed, you know …."

"We work together. She delivers the mail at Micro Silicon. I see her every day. Sometimes twice a day. And we often play racquetball on the weekend."

"Oh. I see. That clarifies *my* confusion. Now back to your confusion … you think that I'm somehow responsible for Bill and Millie?"

"No. Of course not. She's an adult. She learned … whatever she learned. I'm just frustrated that neither of you seemed to see what was patently obvious to me in the first fifteen seconds after I met him. I just don't understand how you could be associated with someone who is so ... unethical."

"Well, I already said. Anyway, I agree with you completely."

Millie came back into the room, carrying a heavily laden tea tray. Michael leaped up and helped her situate it on the bedside table.

"Millie, Michael has just been telling me about how awful Bill was to you, too. I am so, *so* sorry to hear it."

Millie poured tea, but shot Michael a glance. "Oh, well, my problems are nothing compared to what you've gone through. I count my blessings that he dropped me like he did."

"Yes. We all do," Sage agreed, sipping at her tea. "Oh, this is wonderful! What did you do?"

"Boiled water, poured it over tea leaves." Millie handed a tea cup to Michael, who stood awkwardly, holding the cup.

"Well, you did a superlative job of it. I don't think I've ever had tea this delicious."

"I warmed some half and half and poured that in it too. Makes it rich, and will help you relax."

"Lovely. Thank you. Right now it looks like Michael is the one who needs to relax."

"Sit down, Michael," Millie directed.

"Okay." He returned to the love seat.

"What's the matter with you?" she asked.

"Lots of things. Mostly right now, though, I think I did wrong to talk with Sage about you and that nut case."

"No. You did right. Now everything is out in the open. I can't deny that I was taken by him. I really did love to listen to him talk about his work."

"His work as an attorney?" Sage asked, surprised.

"Yes. It was fascinating. I let him talk for hours."

"I can't imagine it! That kind of talk just makes my eyes cross."

"Well," Millie sat on the little bedside chair, blew on her tea, a reflective mood settling on her features, "I was going to be an attorney. I went to law school for two-and-a-half years."

"*What?!*" Sage and Michael exclaimed together.

"Yes. But it was not to be."

"I've never heard a word of this," Michael said, clearly amazed.

"What happened?" Sage asked.

"My mother got sick. My three brothers and sisters were little kids at the time and my dad had checked out long before. I had to come home to take care of the kids. Then ... my mother passed. And, so, that was that. The kids are in college now. Two are in law school. Pretty cool, yes?"

"And you did that?" Sage said in a whisper. "Put them in law school."

"No. I made them work so hard in high school that they got scholarships. I'm no dummy."

"No. Clearly not." Sage looked at Michael, who was looking at Millie like she'd just grown up out of the floor.

"You never told me any of this. You've talked about your siblings. But you never told me any of this. Why didn't you?"

Millie smiled endearingly at Michael. "You've not had this kind of loss. You wouldn't know what it's like. But Sage has had terrible losses. She knows what it's like. Anyway, it's time to let it out."

Sage took hold of Millie's hand. "I'm sorry, Millie. Truly saddened to hear your story. But perhaps there's a silver lining. I know you have a full time job. But would you like a part time job? You just might be the blessing in this whole fiasco. I urgently need someone to make sense of whatever it is that Bill Rattnor has done with Aunt Victoria's estate. Is it of any interest to you to try and sort it out? It's a lot, and maybe it's more than you'd care to take on. But I know Anthony will help you, and I'll do whatever I can, which, frankly, is little more than just—give you a paycheck."

The glow in Millie's eyes let Sage know she was onto something.

"I'd love it! Purely, love it."

"We'll have to see about getting you back on track with law school, too."

"Thank you, Sage. Thank you! I'd give you a hug, but you're too wounded. Virtual hug." Millie hugged herself.

"Virtual hug returned." Sage grinned, even though it hurt.

"Awful warm and fuzzy in here," Anthony said, coming through the door.

"Virtual hugs all around," Sage said, quietly offering up gratitude for her amazing friends.

Chapter 10
Michael

They'd all stayed overnight at Sage's in various guest rooms, retiring after a feast of delivered pizza. Millie and Michael agreed that it was a good thing the next day was Sunday and they didn't have to go to work, plus they could keep an eye on Sage. By Sunday evening, Sage was up and moving about. Stiffly, but on the mend.

After hunkering down over the Petrol-Fill files for a couple of hours with Anthony and Millie, making considerable headway in sorting out the illegal activities of Bill Rattnor, Sage insisted that they get back to their lives, just as she had to get on with hers.

Michael felt increasingly uncomfortable around his uncle's doting on Sage, quietly grateful when they gathered themselves and left, with gentle hugs all around, and Sage promising Anthony she'd call him later that evening.

After dropping Millie off at her home, Michael had never been so relieved to drive into the garage of his little condo. The range of emotions he'd experienced over the previous twenty-four hours wiped him out.

He'd thought that he would go to work and put in a few hours, but as he kicked off his shoes by the back door, he realized he only wanted to be alone. In fact, he wished he were somewhere else altogether. He wanted to get away from everyone. He flung himself onto the sofa, pulled off his horn-rimmed glasses as if they were a weapon and rubbed his eyes.

He even wanted a break from Millie, as much as he cared about her. He wanted time to think about the different person she'd become, now that he knew all these things about her she'd kept from him.

He wanted to have time to consider *himself*. Who was he? he wondered. Someone that his best friend— or so he thought—would not tell him her most important dreams and life goals? Yes, he heard what she'd said, but it didn't wash. Millie had known him for ages and had only recently met Sage.

He dragged himself off the sofa, took a long, hot, shower hoping to fall deep asleep. He hadn't slept even two hours last night between worrying about Sage and trying to get her out of his mind.

And that was the real problem, the core problem, the irritating problem.

He had to get away from Sage. Completely away from her. Just how deeply he'd fallen in love with her in the previous two days he hadn't realized until now, relaxed, showered, in bed. Lonely beyond belief. *Lonely.*

From the moment he looked into those amazing eyes when she rolled down the limo window a crack, until just a couple of hours ago as she waved good-by to them at her front door in an over-sized bathrobe, hair tousled, black eye, face swollen, bruised and bare-footed, she had crawled deeper and deeper into his heart, until there was no deeper place to burrow. The way his feelings for her expanded his heart, he knew it was about to break.

He could quit his job, move back east, return to the life he previously lived. Or he could move to Scotland. He could be contented, ignorant of love.

But it would not be possible. As the proverb said, "A bell once rung cannot be un-rung." The bell of his heart had been rung. Or *wrung*.

If Uncle Anthony and Sage got married ... no, he amended, *when* they got married, Sage would be his aunt and he, Michael, would simply have to learn to get over these feelings for her.

It was plain to see she was calm and happy around Anthony. Uncle Anthony deserved the best. Sage.

After his hot shower and a restless couple of hours sleep, Michael decided to go to work after all. He would work all night and all day tomorrow, bury himself in computer chip anomalies until he dropped. He'd tell his boss tomorrow morning that he needed some time off, then he'd leave for he rest of the week.

He needed to be alone and he needed to be in nature.

*   *

Thea Thomas - 93

After working eighteen hours straight, Michael took off at noon on Tuesday, went home and crashed, with the intention of leaving early the next morning. But he woke up after a few hours feeling an urgency to get on the road. He packed the Audi with tent, sleeping bag, books, gold panning equipment and a folding map of the Southwest, folded open to a highlighted "X" on Gila National Forest.

He drove through the night stopping only for gas. Pre-dawn teased the eastern sky as he headed into the forest. Rolling down the windows, the chilly early morning air bathed him like a tingling shower, and, when he finally stopped at his stream-side destination, stunning shades of orange and pink shot through the sunrise clouds. He stretched his long but cramped and tired legs out of the car, extended his arms toward the horizons, filled with gratitude for all the beauty around him.

Then he heaved a deep, blood-and-pore cleansing sigh.

The line, "if you can't be with the one you love, love the one you're with," crossed his mind. He followed the thought with a wry grin. *Nature* was the one he was with, and he did love her.

In fact, it felt so good to be here in the peace and solitude, a myriad of song birds singing the sun up, the sun warming his sad heart, that he continued to breathe deeply until he became dizzy. He sat, crossed-legged on a large, perfectly flat rock at the edge of the little rushing brook and watched the water, pure and sure of its course, dancing over the rocks.

Why, he wondered, would I ever be in any place other than one like this? The strain of work, of the drive, even of his pre-occupation with Sage, abated and flowed down stream with watching the baptizing water.

Eventually he came out of his meditation, but remaining in a reflective state of bliss he pitched his tent, then arranged rocks into a fire pit, while his raging hunger came on in force. Somewhat surprised, he realized he'd not thought of food since he left his condo.

Now, with the brisk fresh air, his appetite clamped on him with a vengeance. He jumped back into the car, and returned to the truck stop he'd passed. He quickly bought emergency rations; coffee, a few canned goods, a can opener, a loaf of bread, a jar of peanut butter, vegetables, bananas and apples, and grabbed up a novel at the checkout counter, determined to spend as little time around other humans as possible.

Back at his campsite, he wolfed down a couple of peanut butter sandwiches and a can of fruit cocktail. Then he unrolled his sleeping bag under the shade of a leafy tree and slept the sleep of the pardoned.

When he awoke, he watched the sun falling into the western horizon. "Now I'm backwards," he scolded himself. But he didn't care. He got out his lantern and the novel he'd picked up at the truck stop, to read himself back to sleep.

For three days he did nothing but bend over his little stream, panning for gold. He even came up with a few sparkly little bits, although he wouldn't have cared much if he hadn't, he so loved simply hearing the brook bubbling, the birds singing, while feeling the warmth of the sun on his back. For three nights he quickly fell asleep over his book before hardly reading a page. He had yet to even crawl into the tent since he'd befriended the tree by the stream.

The fourth night the near-full moon hovered overhead making sleep impossible. Michael reveled in the stealthy wonderland of the deep shadowed beauty. He panned for gold in the silver moonlight. Hunkering over his pan, little flecks of gold actually sparkled and reflected in the chilled light.

This was living, he thought. Sleeping and waking according to my own, internal clock, responding to the environment. Loving ... no, more than loving, *being* the planet. He tried to remember the last time he felt this happy, relaxed and at peace. Not surprisingly, he recalled it was the last time he went gold panning.

When Michael woke up late the next morning, responsibility tugged at him. He'd soon have to return to civilization. But he felt ready for it. He realized his work was not so much different, really, from gold panning—bending over small things, looking for what was precious.

He soon broke camp and headed back through Flagstaff. He wanted to take a few hours going through the Museum of Northern Arizona, rich with information of the beautiful Southwest and its people.

As he walked into the museum, he was thrilled to see the commitment to Native Americans, hall after hall stretched before him with the promise of untold artifacts.

A little old man at the doorway dressed in a Navajo patterned shirt, and bedecked in turquoise jewelry, looking as though he'd stepped out of one of the exhibits, asked Michael to sign the guest book. Michael signed, glanced over the many books for sale in the gift shop, promising himself that he'd give the books more attention after going through the museum.

He walked down the hall and turned to the first showcase. His heart seemed to stop in his chest, and then banged around so that he had to reach out to hold onto the railing. There before him, was an 11 by 14 inch portrait of Sage, only with brown skin, intense brown eyes and long black hair, holding a beautifully woven basket.

The caption read: "The Elgins did important work in preserving the traditional arts of the Zuni people. It was a great loss to Southwest ethnography when they perished in a small plane crash in the Gila National Forest ...." and text went on.

Michael, glued to the spot, studied the beauty, joy and calmness in the face of Sage's mother. To think he would never meet her, to think that this is who Sage lost, to think that he camped somewhere near where she and her husband, Sage's father, left this world ... he became very nearly overwhelmed.

All the balance he'd regained in the last few days fled, leaving him hollow, disoriented, sad. In the showcase, along with the actual basket that Sage's mother held in the picture, was a display of bright, precious, turquoise, the color of Sage's incredible eyes. He continued to stare at Sage's mother as if he'd put down roots, oblivious to the people passing him, peeking around him at the display. Finally he heard a small boy ask his parents, "What's that man looking at?"

"*Shhh* ... the jewelry," his mother answered, dragging the boy by the hand to the next display.

Michael smiled. Something in him shifted, and he knew he could be friends with Sage, and put the other feelings to rest. She had no family. She needed a brother, not some dopey guy pining for her. She came from a tribal background, where family comes first.

This was the lesson he'd come upon this mecca to learn. To set aside his self-centered thoughts and to love—kindly, unconditionally, *tribally*, if he could even begin to aspire to such selfless heights.

And Sage would soon be family when she and Anthony married.

Michael finally pulled himself away from the picture of Sage's mother and wandered through the rest of the museum. On his way out he bought a book on Zuni art and religious beliefs for himself, and bought a stunning, delicate, silver and turquoise necklace for Sage. He would give her the present after she and Anthony announced their engagement.

Chapter 11
Sage

There was nothing Sage would rather less have to go through than another hearing like the one she'd just endured that put Bill Rattnor away. It had been hellish, and the sooner she could forget it—if she ever could—the happier she'd be.

She wanted to pity him, and, to some extent she had that morning, as he emphatically drove his weird logic in his lawyer voice. Not a single thing he said made sense.

Anthony insisted on going with her, for which she was extremely grateful. His support, ever reliable and his friendship, undemanding. These past few weeks he'd spent many valuable hours away from his own concerns to help her and Millie salvage Victoria's estate.

"How are you feeling?" Anthony asked as they drove away from the courthouse, a place she hoped she'd never have to enter again.

Sage gave him a wan smile. "Glad it's over."

"Me too." He patted her hand. "You look pallid. Have you been eating? Probably not. Let's go to Angelo's for a bit of lunch."

Sage could never thank Anthony enough for staunchly standing by her, but right now she longed to be alone. She'd been coming to this moment, clearing up the mystery, if not the pain, around Aunt Victoria's death, and as much as she cared for Anthony, she needed a private moment.

"Rain check? You're such a dear, Anthony. I know you'll understand. I … I'm … so shaken by his insistence that he's responsible for Aunt Vicky's death—all of that bellowing about having hired a gypsy to put a curse on her …."

"Just lunatic ravings, dear, but I'm so sorry you had to endure it."

"Yes. Lunatic ravings. Of course. But it's …." Sage trailed off. She wanted too, to bring up Rattnor's "lunatic ravings" about Aunt Victoria's and Anthony's relationship—that he had to watch the money disappear when they went off on all their expensive trips together.

As if she'd spoken out loud, Anthony added, "And don't let any of his other ravings bother you, either, Sage. Victoria is gone, may she be in peace. You are here, may you be peaceful and happy, dearest."

Sage nodded. "I'm sure it's best to leave the past where it lies. There are good things I can do—that I desire to do—if, indeed, I'm not poverty-stricken."

"Despite Rattnor's efforts to abscond with every penny of your Aunt's, when all is said and done, I'm sure you'll be quite comfortable. Quite. And can fulfill any desire your sweet heart imagines. I just wish I could take the pain away from you." Anthony reached over and gently patted her shoulder. "But that will come with time."

"I know." Sage turned to look out the window. As they climbed the Canyon Road, she took that as a promise, that her heart would one day climb out of the canyon of her grief. One day, she would be happy again.

Anthony turned onto Sage's driveway, drove up the hill, then stopped the car and walked her to the door.

"Give me a call," he said. "If you don't, I'll send my troops."

"Ah, well, the 'troops' already have an appointment. Millie's coming Sunday. We're spending the day going over the last bit of my handing the baton of Aunt Victoria's businesses over to her."

"*Your* businesses now, dear heart."

"Yes. Well. I'm certainly grateful for Millie's practically mystical appearance in my life. I don't know what I'd do without her. And it's a huge bonus that I simply adore her."

Anthony chuckled. "She *is* relentlessly charming and amusing, I must agree. Okay, I'm away. Don't ...."

"I know, don't hesitate to call." She waved and stepped inside.

As Sage closed the door, she leaned her hands and forehead against it, resisting turning around to face what was now, truly, her home. Her responsibility.

But she did turn. It looked the same. And yet, it looked different. *Her home.* For the first time in her life, she had a place that was truly her own. With a style, furniture and colors all different from what she would choose. But there was one place where she had power, where her choices, and the results of her efforts, were purely her own.

She went up to her room, tore off the stuffy courtroom-appropriate suit and jumped into jeans and work shirt. She twirled her hair up in a big hair clip, noticing that the black eye was nearly gone. She paused and studied her own eyes, the color of a turquoise sky, but where lurked the dark-eyed beauty of her mother. Although her mother's image faded, it could never fully disappear as long as she had a mirror.

She took a moment to thank her ancestors for watching over her in these troubled times. She felt them near. She'd needed to be alone at this moment in order to be with her family. They were here. Sage could feel them now, and became comforted.

To stay close to them, she needed to touch earth. She hurried downstairs, pulled on her mud boots and her now well broken-in garden gloves, then gathered the garden tools and went out to the fragrant, colorful flower garden.

As she stood in the archway of its charming little wooden arbor that she'd repaired and stained the previous week, she surveyed the handiwork she'd accomplished over the past weeks. She'd planted autumn flowers. Now the little green shoots began to poke through the earth. There'd be gigantic bouquets for the house by Thanksgiving, and wonderful autumn flowers in the garden as well.

She could remember many days when she'd stood at her window in her room, watching the gardener doing what she now did. Why had she stood there all those days, lonely and bored, when she could have—*should* have!—been out here?

But Aunt Victoria wouldn't let her do anything that a servant or hired hand was paid to do. She also would not allow Sage to do anything that bore any remote resemblance to her Zuni background. She'd once said that Sage's mother had stolen her brother from her. And she'd said, too, so many times, that Sage was fortunate to have gotten her father's recessive coloring. But she'd always longed to look exactly like her mother, with the dark-yet-kind mystery in the depths of her eyes.

She kept her silence when her aunt got in the mood to criticize her mother. She refused, as much as possible, to hear it. She knew her parents' love was rare. Criticized by family on both sides, they ignored them all and followed their path. In the midst of that incredible love, Sage had been born.

Sage's father, an anthropologist whose work had been to collect and catalog Zuni, Hopi, and Pueblo arts, had put the word out that he needed an assistant.

Her mother was the first applicant for the job. And, as they both told it, they fell in love at first sight.

Sage could remember, as a young child, her father frequently mentioning how he loved it to be away from the freeways and everything else to do with "so-called civilization."

But Aunt Victoria still let Sage know she held more than a grudge against Sage's mother for destroying her plans that her brother would live on a neighboring hill, for stealing him first from her world of wealth, and then for stealing him from the world altogether. In some contorted logic, Aunt Victoria blamed Sage's mother for her brother's death.

Sage tried never to think about how her loyalties were torn, because she loved both her mother and her aunt. But now, while she worked on the dense green ivy, training it over the arbor and cutting it back off the walkways, she allowed herself to mull over the problems her aunt's attitudes had caused her.

What a pity she couldn't have learned to love Sage's mother! Sage vividly remembered the day she flew to Orange County soon after her parents died. After saying a curt hello without even so much as a hug, her aunt launched into a complaint about "those Indians" having the funeral without even inviting her. Sage, having just come from the ceremony, was shocked to hear Aunt Victoria talk openly and critically about the sacred event.

That was only the first of many culture shocks Sage had to endure. Under the veneer she quickly learned to cover herself with, however, she remained Zuni. And now, she'd no longer stifle her roots. She would work in the garden. She would sleep outside under the stars when she felt like it. She would do any earthy, earthly thing she wanted or needed to do.

And she would go to school. She wanted to go back to the reservation. She wanted to pick up where her parents left off, she wanted to help her people preserve their heritage. Since she had a foot in both worlds, she intended to make the best of it by following in her parents' footsteps, majoring in anthropology like her father had.

Sage worked on the flower garden with an unflagging enthusiasm until the sun went down. She fell asleep in a bath of hot water and mineral crystals, exhausted and pleasantly sore-muscled.

When she woke up the next morning, she realized that she'd crawled out of the bath, wrapped a towel around herself and climbed into bed, all in her sleep.

She heard Tina's car rumbling up the drive. Jumping out of bed, she threw on white cotton pants and a pastel print shirt, and stood brushing her hair on the balcony by the time Tina shut off the engine and got out of her VW.

"Hey! You lazy thing!" Tina called from below, "you going to lay around primping all day, or are you ready to get up and do something?"

"What do you have in mind?" Sage called back.

"Let me in! I need some coffee or tea, or something."

Sage ran down the stairs, light-hearted, delighted that Tina had spontaneously arrived. The last time she'd seen her was a couple of days after Rattnor had tried to kill her.

Tina kicked off her shoes at the door and gave her a big hug. "You look fantastic! The black eye is almost completely gone, and you don't look pale as skimmed milk."

"Yes, I'm back to normal—whatever that is!" She chuckled, returning her friend's hug.

The two of them padded barefoot to the kitchen. Tina perched on a kitchen stool while Sage put together a bit of breakfast.

"I've been working on the flower garden," Sage pointed with a large slotted spoon through the window. "Yesterday I trained the ivy over the arbor, and tended to the amazing roses."

"I *see* ... very charming, Sage! It *was* becoming kind of an eyesore. But don't overdo it. You're still healing."

"I take it easy. Rake a bit, sit a bit, plant a bit, listen to birds a bit. It's extremely therapeutic and makes me so happy, even though the whole thing with Bill Rattnor ...."

"So what *happened* at the hearing with that creep, anyway?"

"He's pretty over the edge. Nothing he says makes sense. His doctor testified and said Bill had a psychotic break. Which anyone can see without being told. In any case, he's under lock and key and no longer a worry of mine.

"But, as I mentioned, the good news has been that not only are my finances not in the state of total ruin that they first appeared to be, Millie has turned out an absolute godsend. She's brilliant and is always one step ahead of me as we're sorting through the muddle Rattnor made of Aunt Vicky's estate. He certainly did succeed in spending a sizable amount of her money in a surprisingly short while. I don't care. I don't need to be rich, I just want to be organized."

"I'm glad that the surprise about Millie's 'hidden talents' is working out for both of you. That means you can stop worrying about all the stuff and come out to play."

Sage laughed. "Well, something like, I guess." She poured boiling water into the tea pot. "I can get a more reasonable car. In fact, let's go car shopping. That's sort of like play, isn't it?"

"Big kid play, yes, indeedy!" Tina agreed.

Sage piled all the breakfast goodies on a tray and led the way to the breakfast nook, Tina following with dishes and silverware. They sat facing the window to admire the reincarnating garden.

"I also thought," Tina said,"that you and I might register for classes."

"Mind reader! Just last night I decided to go back to school—major in anthropology. I want to pick up where my parents left off and work with my tribe."

"Like you've always wanted to," Tina observed.

"How do you know?"

"I *do* listen when you talk, Sage. Over the years you've said a lot of things."

"But I didn't even decide this myself until yesterday, with my hands in the earth of the garden."

"You didn't put the pieces together, but it's all been there. You just needed freedom to let yourself see it."

"You're awesome."

After a few moments of reflective silence, Tina said softly, "So, from *things* you're interested in, to *people* you're interested in ... what do you hear of Michael lately?"

"You mean the person *you're* interested in, don't you?" Sage teased.

"Let's be perfectly honest ... a person we're both interested in."

They giggled.

"I *do* have a bit of information about him," Sage said. "With all the dramatic events swirling around, I completely forgot to tell you. He's not involved with Millie in a romantic way. They're friends. She delivers the mail at Micro Silicon."

"You forgot to tell me *that*?"

"Well, it's been ...."

"Crazy, I understand."

"Yes. Crazy." Sage agreed.

Tina leaned back in her chair, twirling a lock of her long brown hair. Her green eyes sparkled. "What are you going to do about him?"

"What am I going to 'do' about him?" Sage shook her head. "Nothing. I don't chase men. in any case, I've got too much to attend to right now. He appears to dislike me."

"Who appears to dislike you?" Tina asked, confused.

"Michael!" Sage answered. "Michael doesn't like me. I don't know why, but he always seems to be angry with me. No, angry is too strong. He always seems to be just ... *peeved* with me. The first night I met him he clearly thought I was an idiot. In his defense, I did have the limo all across the road. And then, well, maybe it's chemistry, but he just does *not* like me."

Sage paused, then went on, "I think he has some attitude about Anthony and me. I don't know, maybe he thinks I'm after his uncle's money ...."

Tina grunted. "Phooey. That's easily cleared up. Anyone who knows you, knows you care about people, not money."

"But on the other hand, Tina, I don't feel I should *have* to clear it up. If someone thinks of me that way, well, they can just have that opinion."

"Biting off your nose to spite your own lovely face. Always an interesting approach," Tina observed.

"Anyway, I have all these things to do ...."

"Okay. I hear the excuses. For some reason, you don't want to do anything about the only man I've ever seen you actually interested in. I won't nag you anymore about it." Tina paused. "Can I have him?"

Sage laughed then shrugged. "Sure, you can have him if he's to be had—I'm in no position to give him away. I wish you all the luck in the world. He's wonderful to look at, but seems difficult to get along with. I leave it up to you to find that out for yourself."

Sage stood and started to clear the breakfast dishes. "In the meantime, let's get moving on all our projects. Can I go dressed this casually?"

"Perfect, as always. Let's hit the road."

Chapter 12
Michael

Michael answered his phone distracted, mind on his work.

"Hi, gorgeous!" Came a cheerful yet unfamiliar voice.

"Hello," he answered, flagging a potential trouble spot on the computer chip diagram he worked on.

"How's life treating you?"

"Over-worked, but fine." Why isn't this person identifying herself? he wondered, continuing to track down the error in the diagram.

"Sounds like you need a break. Why don't you meet me for lunch?"

"Millie?" As soon as he said it, he knew he was wrong. There was nothing about Millie in this woman's voice.

"No. Sorry, it's Tina."

Michael was blank.

"Sage's friend ... you met me at Anthony's party ...."

"Oh, yes, now I remember." Michael finally put down his concentration on his work, his train of thought destroyed. "What ... why are you calling?"

"I thought we might go to lunch. I'd like to talk with you about a couple of things."

"Talk about a couple of things? What ... what things?" Michael answered, completely mystified.

"Oh, well, if it's that taxing to spend some time with me ...."

Then he realized that Tina might want to talk about Sage. "I'm sorry, Tina," Michael's tone softened. "I've been really over-extended at work. I have a difficult time shifting gears. I think I'm with you now."

"Great! Let's start over ... would you like to go to lunch?"

"Okay. When?"

"Is today ...."

"Today isn't good," Michael's gaze returned to the computer chip, "but tomorrow works, if it's good for you."

"Excellent. Do you know Monterey Bay Cannery?"

"Yes ...that's one place I happen to know."

"Noonish?"

"Okay."

"Will you recognize me?" Tina asked.

"I think so. I recall you have very long, dark, hair."

"Right. I'll stand with my back to the door." She giggled endearingly. "See you tomorrow. Bye."

Michael chuckled as he hung up, then entered a note on his calendar.

*   *

The next day Michael came into the restaurant at twelve-thirty. He'd completely forgotten his luncheon date—until the alarm went off on his phone.

Harried, he abandoned his work and dashed to the restaurant. He ran into the restaurant, looking for long dark hair, when someone touched his elbow.

He turned to look into two huge green eyes.

"Hi," Tina said in a cool, collected voice.

"Hi," Michael answered, "Tina?"

"Very good. You remembered my name."

"Yes, I remember your name, I just don't remember your face. That is, I don't remember you looking like this."

Tina, a tanned goddess, her long hair shining with highlights, wore a jade green Hawaiian print strapless sun dress. She was cool as mint julep.

"Not too flattering, considering you were looking right at me while I taught you how to waltz."

"Don't take my boorishness for an insult, please!" Michael protested. "I'm afraid I was primarily looking at your feet ... or mine while struggling with the waltz. Anyway, I apologize for being late, I ... I'm ... work has me ...."

"That's all right." Tina waved his apology aside. "I got a table by the window, ordered a glass of wine and watched for you to come. I thought you might not."

Michael wondered at being considered someone who would not keep an appointment. But she was right. If not for the alarm on his phone, he would have inadvertently stood her up.

Tina led the way to a secluded booth. A giant reed ceiling fan turned lazily overhead. Michael felt himself relaxing.

"I don't care for this August heat," Michael reached to loosen his tie, then realized he hadn't worn one.

Tina smiled at him languidly. "Personally, I'm rather like a lizard. I'm perfectly happy to stretch out on a rock and let the sun put me to sleep on a day like this." She stretched her long arms in a lizard-like imitation.

"While us androids slave away in air-conditioned office buildings," Michael noted.

"Something like that. But I'm giving the wrong impression. I work too, I'm on vacation now."

"I see." Michael was trying to equate this woman with the girl who had accompanied Sage to Uncle Anthony's party.

Tina gestured to a carafe on the table. "I took the liberty of ordering a nice wine. Would you like some?" Tina asked.

"I don't usually drink during the work day."

"I have three things to say about that. One, one should once in a while break one's own rules just to show oneself who's boss, two, a little wine is good for the digestion, and three, it's not nice to make a lady drink alone."

"Hmmm," Michael pondered. "The last two points I'll accept, the first one I'm not too sure about."

"Doesn't matter," Tina said, filling Michael's wine glass.

The young, California-blonde waitress in crisp white short-shorts and a bright Hawaiian shirt with a hot-pink lei came and took their order.

"So," Michael said when she left, running his fingers through his tousled hair, "what are these subjects you need to discuss with me?"

"Going right for business!"

"I thought you'd appreciate it," Michael answered.

"Not exactly. I'd kind of like to have a bit of chit-chat until at *least* after the salad."

"Really?" Michael asked, puzzled. "What could you possibly have to say to me that you can't just come right out with?"

"Oh. Well ... well, if that's the way you want it. I wanted to discuss you and me," Tina blurted.

"You and me?"

"Surely, Michael, you've had women interested in you before, you don't *really* have to act so ... blank."

Michael raised his eyebrows. You're dense, Michael, he said to himself. "I'm sorry, Tina. I really missed the whole point. I thought you must have something you felt you needed to discuss about Sage, or perhaps my uncle ... or something along those lines. Because, you know, that's all we have in common. I didn't think ...."

The waitress brought their salads. Tina was half-grinning at Michael's awkward efforts to pull himself out of the mire he dug himself deeper into.

"I should have known ... once any man has seen Sage, I just don't exist."

"It's not like that, Tina. I'm simply saying that I could only assume you felt we needed to talk about what we have in common, that is, those two people. To the best of my understanding, he and Sage are headed for matrimony. Sage is a nice woman, and my uncle cares deeply about her." Michael stopped—defensive, sweating, and feeling guilty. Which he hated.

"Wow, Michael," Tina responded cooly. She picked at her salad. "But now you *do* know why I wanted to see you." She put down her salad fork and leaned toward Michael, her large green eyes compelling, a waft of her sensual perfume enveloped him. "I'd like to get to know you. I'd like us to be friends." She leaned back into the booth.

"I appreciate your honesty," Michael answered too quickly. "But," he continued more slowly, "you've really, ah, shocked me."

Tina shrugged as if nothing in the world mattered one way or the other. "Let's start over. I'll tell you a bit about me, you tell me a bit about you. I'll tell a couple of jokes that I memorized for the occasion, you'll laugh as though you're charmed.

"And then, if you feel so inclined, when the waitress asks us if we want dessert, and I say oh no, I couldn't, and you say, no thanks, just some coffee, please, then you can turn to me and say, well, Tina, this was a pleasant enough interlude from work, but really, I find you an unlikable homely witch, and I'd consider myself lucky to never encounter you again by even the remotest of accidents."

Michael grinned. "You're a character!"

The waitress brought the main course and they both fell to devouring it. Michael was quiet while Tina regaled him with a long and convoluted story about a man searching for the greatest swordsman in all the world. She was an entertaining story-teller and he often found himself with fork poised in mid-air for a punch line.

He felt wonderfully relaxed ... he hadn't let his tensions go like this in amusement and a couple of glasses of wine in many a month. Maybe even years, he thought. Because it seemed that the women he dated were only interested in being told how beautiful they were. Even Millie, though a good friend and companion, always expected Michael to repair her broken or wounded ego or to pat her on the back or to tell her what to do.

He sincerely doubted that this animate woman across the table *could* be told what to do.

Before he knew it, the waitress had removed their plates and was asking them if they wanted dessert, Tina was saying that she couldn't possibly and Michael caught himself saying no thanks, just some coffee, when he glanced at Tina and they both burst out in a giggle.

"I'm sorry," Michael apologized to the waitress, "we just had a .... *deja vu,* I guess you might say. And to break the curse, I believe I'll have a piece of cheese cake."

"What the heck," Tina said, "me too." The waitress walked away, shaking her head. "So you're not going to call me a witch?" Tina asked him.

"Bewitching. But definitely not a witch."

"Do you think something could happen between us?"

"I think we can be good friends. But I won't mislead you, Tina, I'm not interested in a relationship right now. I'm too committed to my work."

"All my charm for naught!" Tina complained.

"I don't know how to answer that. I like you a lot, but I … don't have time for a relationship right now. I wouldn't be able to give a relationship what I think it deserves."

"I wish you'd let me decide that ... let me tell you, after a trial run, if I think you don't have enough to give."

Michael reached across and patted Tina's hand. "Tina, you're wonderful, you really are. Witty and pretty and utterly likable. I'm happy to have had this lunch with you. Thank you for dragging me out of my dungeon, and I'd love to do it again. But that's about all it could be."

"I guess I ought to be pleased that you don't think I'm a horrible stupid brazen wench. Here's my number, Michael. Call anytime you want to talk. Or, rather, blabber mouth that I am, any time you want to be *talked to*."

"It's a deal."

On the way back to work, an hour late, Michael asked himself why he was so adamant in turning Tina down. A guy could look long and hard to find a woman that bright and cute and charming and cheerful.

But the "chemistry," wasn't there. He knew that feeling, and he knew where it was—how he hated to admit it!—he felt it every time he saw Sage.

Chapter 13
Sage

Sage, covered in more pale cocoa-brown paint on herself than she succeeded in getting on the wall, answered her phone, giving it lovely cocoa fingerprints. She saw Tina's number. "What's up?"

"I did it."

"Did what?" Sage wracked her brain for things Tina recently threatened to do. "Do I have to guess, or can I give up right away?" she chuckled.

"Oh, Sage, it's not funny! I've made a complete fool of myself and did something I've *never* done. Not that I've never made a fool of myself ...."

"Tina!"

"I ... I asked Michael out."

Sage plopped down on the stairway, stunned. "You asked Michael out? And you're mortified? What *happened?*"

"He was so nice, so polite. Completely Mr. Manners. But he only went to lunch with me because he thought I had something to say about you and Anthony."

"Anthony and me—as a couple?"

"I don't know. I didn't spend a lot of time dwelling on the reasons I *didn't* ask him out. When he said he'd go to lunch with me I thought it was because he was interested in me. I'm a nit-wit."

"Stop, Tina. There could be so many reasons why he ... I don't even know what he did. What did he do?"

"He was an angel."

"He's clearly a terrible person ...."

"I'm so embarrassed to have chased him. He said he didn't have time for romance in his life right now. He said his work comes first. He said he wouldn't be able to commit to a relationship. Practically word for word what you've said—the two of you are made for each other. Except you both think your time is too precious to share. When I think of all the people in the world dying for romance and the two of you are too 'busy' for love."

"I suppose neither he nor I have found the person we can fall in love with."

"Whatever. All I know is, I'll never be able to face that man again."

"Nonsense. He's not an ogre. I'm sure he's flattered. And I'm sure he likes you. Everybody likes you, Tina. He didn't fall in love with you. So what? It just makes you one more person closer to your perfect person. Can you paint?"

"Huh?"

"I'm painting a wall, but there's more paint on me, the floor, and now my cell phone than the wall."

"Yeah, okay, I'll come over and help you out of your mess."

"And I'll help you out of yours. Not that you're in a mess. I think we need to change the environment. Given that Millie has put my financial house in order and I have some mad money, I've been thinking about going away for a few days. But I can't decide where to go. Where would you like to go?"

"Am I going with you?"

"I hope so. I don't want to go alone."

"*Oooooh*, goody! You already know my obsession."

"Steel drums."

"Yes."

"Reggae."

"Yes."

"Jamaica."

"Yes."

"You'll be swamped with men. This time next week you'll be saying, 'Michael who?'" Sage said.

"Are you serious about this?"

"Completely, utterly, serious. But please do come over and help me. Wear clothes you'd like to be a lovely shade of brown."

"I'm there. We can paint and plan."

"Besides," Sage added, "maybe after thinking about you for a while, Michael will change his mind."

"You always find the silver lining."

"If you look for the good, the good shows up."

*   *

A week later, Sage and Tina had taken a flight to Jamaica, and sat looking at the ocean, drinking sodas on the lanai of their two bedroom suite in Kingston. The enchanting tones of steel drums reverberated up to them from the street, an offering of peace and pleasure.

"Paradise!" Tina exclaimed.

"Paradise," Sage agreed lazily.

"Let's go out!" Tina jumped up and started rummaging through her luggage.

"Don't you want to relax for a while?"

"Nope! We're only here five days, I don't want to miss a minute!"

"You go ahead. I think I can afford to miss a few minutes. I came for the music, and the way it's floating up from the street is heaven." Sage yawned. "I need to take a little nap."

"I don't want to go out alone," Tina whimpered.

"Stay in the hotel. There's lots to do. Go down to the lounge. Give me a call in a couple hours, or come and get me."

Tina brightened. "Okie-dokie! See you later."

Sage stretched out on the bed, thinking about her determination that Tina see she was attractive to men. "If I have to push her out of the nest with both wings!" she said as she drifted off to sleep, her dreams woven with reggae. When her phone woke her up with Tina's ring, she was dancing in a dream with Michael, their bodies synchronized with the lilting syncopated beat of the music from the street.

"Wake up! Come down!" Tina shouted over a reggae band. "These men are gorgeous and fantastic dancers."

"What time is it?" Sage looked around for a clock, it was too dark to see her watch.

"You've been sleeping for hours! I just haven't been able to tear myself away. But now I've got more men than I can handle. I need you."

"I won my bet."

"What?" Tina shouted over the din.

"I won my bet!" Sage shouted back.

"Oh, yeah! Absolutely! I fe-e-el to-toooo coul, m-a-a-n," Tina giggled. "Come on!"

"Okay. I'll be right down."

Sage changed into a red silk pantsuit and headed for the music. She and Tina danced until the sun came up, then went back up to the room and slept like logs until late afternoon.

They ordered gigantic salads brought to their suite, then sat on the lanai enjoying the pristine view. Tina glowed. "Nothing like *men* to make a girl forget a man!" she said in happy contemplation.

"Umm." Sage felt disoriented and exhausted after hours of even more insistent dreaming about Michael. She couldn't remember the dreams, but she saw his face in her mind's eye, and felt his presence. This trip was supposed to take her *away* from these haunting thoughts. But distance had no influence on where the heart would go.

"Poor imitation of enthusiasm, Sage."

"Sorry. My mind is ...."

"Somewhere else, I can see that. Where?"

"I'm thinking about what I'd like to do this afternoon. I think I'll rent a car and drive around the country. How does that sound to you?"

"Fine, as long as we're back by party-time tonight."

"Party time. Well, I guess we could take a scenic drive for a few hours. I'm not going to party all night tonight though, I want to go sight-seeing tomorrow, so don't be surprised when I disappear early, and leave at the crack of dawn tomorrow."

*   *

Sage didn't mind at all the next day when Tina was no more able to go sight-seeing at eight a.m. after three hours sleep than she could get up and fly. Sage gathered her camera and notebook, threw a dark scarf over her hair and put on large, dark, sunglasses, wanting to see rather than be seen.

She ran elatedly downstairs, jumped into her little rented car and took off for *Ocho Rios*. She'd gathered fliers at the hotel lobby, and now she couldn't wait to get to the *Coyaba River Garden and Museum*, only about an hour away.

Once there, she sat contentedly for an hour by the Mahoe Falls, the water tripping and dancing down the rock stairs of the falls. It cleared her head in a calming and spiritual way, after which she went through the Coyaba museum, and felt, finally, *finally!* as though she'd arrived at this island paradise.

When she got back in her little car, she drove to Port Antonio, looking forward to going through the *Nonsuch Caves*, which, the literature said, "were a series of fourteen chambers with bizarre rock formations, speleothems and Arawak Indian drawings, with a bat colony living in the thirteen meter high, gothic-shaped ceiling of the Cathedral Chamber. The caves were discovered by a lost goat in 1957."

Sage wondered how the goat found its way back out. But even more importantly, she hoped she'd learn how the goat managed to tell people about the caves!

Simply put, the *Nonsuch Caves* promised to be many things Sage loved to experience, all-in-one: caves, bats, and ancient rock drawings. But when she arrived, she was profoundly disappointed to discover that the caves were now closed to the public. She had to console herself with meandering through the botanical garden above the caves, imagining what lay beneath, as she wandered through a wonderland of exotic plants and breath-taking butterflies, dragonflies, birds.

Finally she climbed back into her trusty little rental and drove on around the eastern point of Jamaica, feeling that, whatever else she did while here, this day she'd fulfilled her dreams—to be in nature, to feel the warmth of another place find a lovely spot to curl up in, in her mind. It would remain there, always.

Returning to her Americanized hotel, discordant with the surrounding, natural beauty, and the natural people she'd chatted with in her travels that day, she felt resistance. Dragging her feet, she went to her room. A note from Tina rested on her pillow, saying she'd gone to dinner with someone named Alfred.

At that moment the hotel phone rang.

"It's me," Tina called cheerfully. "When'd you get back?"

"This very minute." Sage sank into a chair.

"Well, get on over here. I'm at a place you'll just love. Little outdoor restaurant by the ocean, local food like you can't believe, a steel drum band on loan from heaven ... they're on a break, so I thought I'd call when I could hear you."

"Sounds great. Where are you?"

"I'm going to have Alfred send a cab for you. The driver will know where to come."

"Who's Alfred?" The band started up in the background, drowning out any ability to talk. "I have to shower and change," Sage shouted. "How long did it take you to get there?"

"About twenty minutes."

"Okay. Tell the cab driver to get me in half-an-hour. I'll see you soon."

Her mood shifted to one of anticipation. After her quick shower, she put on a white, full-skirted dress and brushed her loose-hanging hair. Then she ran down and got in the waiting cab. The driver took her through the darkening shadows among narrow streets.

After a while, however, she realized that they surely had been driving longer than twenty minutes. She looked at her watch. She'd give the driver another ten minutes before saying anything.

The ten minutes passed, and still they drove on, nothing like a restaurant in sight.

"Driver," Sage finally spoke up. He did not respond. "Driver, why aren't we there? We should be at the restaurant by now."

"Soon miss, we'll be there soon."

"I hope so." Sage sat back, tense, fear creeping up her esophagus.

The car wound about narrow streets so dark it was difficult for Sage to see where the street was. Then, suddenly, they stopped in front of a small, dark, cottage, the driver turned off the ignition.

"This is not a restaurant," Sage said to him.

He got out, came around the car, opened Sage's door.

"This is not a restaurant, and I'm not getting out."

"Please, please do get out miss."

"No. Take me back to the hotel."

A small light came on in the cottage, someone's head peeked through a window. Sage's heart began to race. What was she to do now?

"Please get out of the car, miss." The driver stood politely by the door. Sage thought about attempting to leap from the car, but where would she go?

"I *insist* that you take me either back to the hotel, or to the restaurant. Maybe you're lost," Sage went on, "maybe you don't know where the restaurant is. That's okay. Just take me back to the hotel."

"I know where the restaurant is, my cousin is the cook there. Excellent cook. We be there soon, sooner if you please get out, I want you to meet someone."

Heart pounding, she slowly climbed out of the car. Perhaps there was someone here that she could appeal to. The driver touched her elbow and escorted her to the door of the cottage. He opened the door, but she flatly refused to go through it by anything less than brute force.

The face at the window came to the door. The driver and the young woman exchanged a few quiet words. Then, suddenly, the whole cottage was full of light, the doorway crowded with women. They came out to Sage and coaxed her inside, speaking in a beautiful liquid language that Sage felt as though she should be able to understand, but couldn't.

"My family, miss," the driver said over the din, grinning from ear to ear. "My four sisters, two cousins, and my mother. I wanted them to see your amazing hair."

The girls were all smiling at her, they lightly touched her sleeve, her arm, her cheek, her hair, giggling and huddling together.

One of the older ones came up to Sage. "My brother is fun, is he not? He works all day, all night for the money we live on, but takes the time to share his uptown life. The girls," she gestured to her little sisters and cousins, "love to see the expensive ladies ... even from far away."

She turned to her brother. "Thank you brother, now take this nice lady to where she was going." She said something to the girls and they all stepped back. Her driver whisked her back into the taxi and pulled onto the road.

Sage, still in a whirlwind of surprise, felt tears in her eyes for the touching scene of this quiet man taking her to see his family, the only entertainment he could afford.

"You have a lovely, sweet family," she said to him.

"Thank you, miss. I know. Though I will be glad when they start to get married so that one day perhaps *I* can afford to get married, and have my own life."

He pulled up in front of another cottage, this one brightly lit, with colored lanterns hanging everywhere and steel drums pulsing in the night air.

"Here we are, miss." He opened her door. As she stepped out she saw Tina waving.

She gave the driver a sizable tip. "Tell your family that I think they are wonderful and beautiful. They're incredibly fortunate to have you watch over them."

"Thank you, miss. Thank you very much."

She watched him drive away.

Tina ran up to her. "You're late! I called your phone, no answer, then I called the room. I thought maybe you decided to go to sleep. Still no answer—I was worried!"

"Well, I was too, for a while, but it came out okay," Sage answered.

"What do you mean?"

"I'll tell you about it later."

"Okay. Come, I want you to meet Alfred." Tina led her to a slightly balding, slightly rotund man. Not at all what Sage expected. Tina immediately cleared up the mystery. "Alfred's a talent scout. He's looking for the next Bob Marley. He knows the music better than most of the musicians themselves. We got to talking and—he's just so fun to hang out with."

Sage shook Alfred's hand, then Tina introduced her to about twenty other people she'd met that evening, including the members of the band. Sage had to admit one thing, Tina could remember people's names like no one she'd ever known. She had clearly become the darling of everyone here.

The music, itself, insisted that Sage dance, which she did until she nearly dropped. Finally she moved to the sidelines and watched her friend. There was no stopping Tina! It warmed the cockles of her heart to see her truly in her element.

As she listened to the music, she closed her eyes and let it embrace her. A young woman who had been introduced as Angie came and stood by her. "My sister, she runs a beauty parlor, you ought to have her do your hair."

"Oh, I don't usually 'do' anything with my hair," Sage answered.

"My sister do it up in cornrows, beads, you'll look like a goddess. You have that face."

"Cornrows? I don't know. I don't know if I *do* have that kind of face." She smiled at Angie. "But I'm curious how it would look."

Tina joined them, perspiring and fanning herself.

"What do you think, should I get my hair done in cornrows?" Sage asked.

"Oh yes! It'll be amazing!"

"Maybe I'll try it ... why not? And you too, Tina."

"Nope, not me."

"Why not?" Sage asked.

"I had it done once. Have you ever given a cat a bath, you know how ludicrous they look when they're completely wet? That's how *I* look with my hair in cornrows."

Sage and Angie laughed.

"I'm serious," Tina protested. "It's like I was slapped with an ugly board."

"Well, I still think I'll try it," Sage said. "Give me the address, Angie."

For the rest of the night Sage watched the svelte dark limbs of the dancers and listened to the mellow bright tones of the steel drums, and thought, "this is nirvana."

*   *

The following afternoon Sage relaxed in a chair while her hair was braided and beaded into cornrows, the soft language of the women coming and going, flowing over her like a healing mineral stream.

"Your hair is not thin and lazy like much blonde hair," Dahlia, Angie's sister, said as she deftly braided. "It is strong. Has strength like good black hair. Special hair, strong, blonde. And you too, a strong woman. I can feel grief coming out through you, girl. But you're strong."

Sage's brow furrowed at these words. Here, in this mystical place with the wonderful people she'd met, she was just about the happiest she'd been since a child. And yet, her grief still came off her?

"I tell you something else I know ... there's a good man, a young man, at home for you. He waits. You here, you try to forget. Okay. Fine. You need to forget *for a while.* You get back, you *remember.*"

"Hmm." Sage said thoughtfully, "why do you say this personal thing about me?"

"I'm touching you for hours. I feel everything come out of you and go toward you. I feel it all."

After a few hours, Dahlia handed Sage a mirror.

Sage gasped. "It's ... it's stunning!"

Dahlia nodded. "Yes. So unusual when my sister recommend someone to come see me, especially foreigners. Just locals. But she knows what she sees when she sends someone to me. She's very particular. *I'm* very particular. I hate to do hair I'm not liking.

"Never mind all that. You listen to what I say now. This good young man, the one who wears glasses," she made two round circles with her fingers before her huge brown eyes, "you don't keep him waiting. Good man deserve good treatment. Good men are special."

"That's true," Sage agreed, "good men are special."

Sage had left Tina sleeping soundly when she went to Dahlia's. As she drove back to the hotel, she had her mind on what Dahlia had said, entirely oblivious of the ripple of attention she created with her bright blonde, long, braided and beaded, hair.

"Oh wow, Sage," Tina exclaimed, eyes wide when Sage walked into their suite. "Look at you! Hollywood, eat your dust!"

Sage laughed.

"I'm not kidding—all those gold filigree and turquoise beads, you look like you're wearing a crown! Queen Sage!" Tina bowed her head.

"Enough groveling, oh faithful servant," Queen Sage said. "Put down that toast. I'm starving! Let's go find a real meal and put on a couple of pounds. We're only here two more days."

"Oh, you're a good queen." Tina went into her room and got into a pair of jeans and a tube top.

Sage called from the lanai, "You won't believe what Dahlia told me."

Tina popped back into Sage's room. "What?"

As they wandered down the hall to the stairs, Sage told her what Dahlia had said about the "good young man."

"Michael," Tina affirmed as they stepped out into the bright late afternoon sun.

Sage shrugged.

"Not just a shrug, Sage. She picked up on the truth. The two of you ought to be together. It's just when you said you didn't want him that I ... you know ... I didn't want him to go to waste. I wanted to keep him in the 'family.'"

"What I said was ...."

"That he's a challenge."

"Yes. He seems challenging. But, the thing is, the *strange* thing is, I keep having all these dreams about him ...."

Tina stopped short. "You didn't tell me that!"

"I know. I didn't want to bother you. I didn't want to bring him up. But he appears anyway. And I'm having dreams with him in them. Every night and every time I take a nap. Just, *always.* It's driving me kind of crazy. I'd hoped that here, changing my environment, changing everything, the dreams would leave me alone. But no, it hasn't worked out that way at all. The dreams have been more incessant and insistent here than at home."

"He's thinking about you."

"I don't know. That would be strange, wouldn't it? When he's so testy and unfriendly?"

"He's testy and unfriendly because he doesn't want to face his feelings for you. Because of Anthony."

"Yes. Well. Anthony. Another sticky wicket."

"Sage, my friend, you can't live other people's lives. It's quite enough to live your own and do right by it. Anthony will be fine, whatever happens."

"You're right."

They stopped in front of a cheerful restaurant, with yellow and white umbrellas over the outside tables, yellow and white checked table clothes, and a yellow and white cat, sitting in a window box, full of happy yellow daisies.

"This is the place," Tina said.

"Definitely!" Sage nodded.

During their perfect, delicious, people-watching-and-being-watched-luncheon—Sage's brilliant hair continuing to cause people to walk into one another when passing, the cat came and purred at their ankles.

The two remaining days in paradise passed all too quickly.

Chapter 14
Michael

Mr. Allerton came into Michael's office, barely knocking, and certainly not waiting for an answer. "I need you to go to the Bay area," he said without preamble. "I want you to work with the guys at the production plant, see if we can't iron out a couple problems cropping up with that chip before they get out of hand."

"What about this one?" Michael pointed to the plans spread out before him.

"I'll put a couple of the guys here on it. I need you where I need you, and unfortunately, you can't be in two places at once. I'd clone you if I could. Anyway, I've got to have you up there tomorrow."

"Well, at least you've given me some notice." Michael's tone was droll.

"You're welcome," Mr. Allerton replied in similar tone as he turned and left Michael's office.

Michael did not like having to switch mental gears with his work, and his boss knew it. There must be *major* problems with the chip in production in Silicon Valley. Another minus because he did not enjoy trying to discover where someone else had glitched up his carefully designed work.

The next day, as he waited in line to rent a car at the San Francisco airport, he suddenly remembered that his Aunt Alison had moved to San Francisco after divorcing Anthony. Maybe he could find her. She'd always been his favorite aunt, and, as a child, he knew nothing of "aunt by marriage." When they divorced, he didn't understand why he never saw her again.

He wasn't sure that he even understood it now.

But the crazy week with the failing computer chip didn't allow him a moment to sleuth out where his aunt might be. He struggled with production problems during fourteen hour days in the lab, going out to lunch and dinner with lab personnel, discussing chip problems, dragging himself to the impersonal hotel late at night to fall down on the bed puzzling over chip problems.

He wondered why he didn't just buy a sleeping bag and sleep on the floor of the production lab from two to six a.m. He'd save the company some money and himself commute time.

It wasn't until the weekend when a couple of his coworkers insisted on spending time with wives and children that his memory was jogged, and he recalled his resolve to look up his Aunt Alison.

"Are you ready to put in a long weekend," one of the team asked Michael during lunch.

"No, Bob, I'm not. I've got an aunt in San Francisco, and I hope to spend some time with her."

"While some of us are working our tails off all weekend," Bob said, voice edgy.

"And I hope you enjoy yourselves immensely. But I've put in a sixty-five hour week, and I'm taking a break."

"Yeah, burn out," Bob observed.

Michael shrugged. "I realize this is a pretty revolutionary notion, but why don't you all take the week-end off? And come refreshed on Monday morning."

Bob's eyebrows went up almost into his hairline. "Yeah? But what would I do all weekend?"

Michael chuckled. "Well, I *do* have something to do. I haven't seen this aunt since I was about thirteen."

"Well, that's different then. You know, maybe I *will* take Sunday off. Do something unheard of, like read a newspaper, if they still have them, or maybe I'll go see a movie. Do you know if they still have movies?"

"Yeah, rumor has it there are still movies out there somewhere. You might even ask a girl to go with you."

Bob feigned shock. "A girl? I'm not sure I'd recognize one if she came up and nibbled my ear. Although nothing like that has happened to me in longer than I can remember. What about you, Michael? You're a good looking guy. Have you had any girls nibbling your ear lately?"

"Nope," Michael answered, continuing the mood, but suddenly finding images of Sage in his mind. "No movies or ear nibbling for me either. We're just a couple of nerds, Bob."

"*Urg!* Right to my face! Have you no mercy?"

"Somebody's got to let you know."

"Thanks, pal. You may have done me a huge favor. Maybe I'll be happily married and working only eight to five come Monday morning, just because you told me these wonderful truths. I'd owe a life of happiness to you."

"They exchanged a glance. "*Naw!*"

Late that night Michael dragged himself to his hotel room. He'd worked from six-thirty that morning until eleven at night. But he felt cheerful. Tomorrow he'd spend with his Aunt Alison, if he could find her. He passed out in a deep, and for once, a non-computer chip filled, sleep.

*   *

In the morning he did an internet search for Alison Williamson, but the only person who came up was an artist, who had quite a few show and was, apparently, fairly famous. Disappointed, he wondered if she took her maiden name back, or even, perhaps, she'd remarried. Or moved away.

How could he track her down? Anthony might have information about her, but neither he nor Anthony had ever brought her up since Michael moved out to the coast, and Michael had no idea what his uncle felt about his ex-wife. He didn't want to find out it was negative.

He called his mother to see if she knew anything about Alison.

The first thing she said was, "What's wrong?" It was true that he rarely called. The three hour time difference made it difficult—by the time he got home at night, it was too late to call her.

"Nothing. Everything's fine. I'm in Northern California working on a project. How's everything at your end?"

His mother assured him everything was fine and then prattled on about various members of the family and her dog.

"The reason I'm calling, mom," Michael finally got in edge-wise, "is because I was wondering ... I'm in San Francisco and I know that's where Aunt Alison was living. I was thinking about looking her up. I can't seem to find her. The only Alison Williamson is this rather famous artist ... do you know anything about her? Did she take her maiden name, did she get re-married?"

"She's sent me a couple of Christmas cards over the years. Let me get my address book, and see what I have for her."

A moment later his mother gave him the last address for Aunt Alison's she'd gotten on a Christmas card several years previous. After saying good-by to his mother, he googled the address. It came up as belonging to A. Williamson, with a phone number attached. Not anticipating success, he dialed the number.

"Hello?" A sweet voice answered. Although he'd never heard his aunt say much, he immediately recognized her voice.

"Is this Alison Williamson?"

"Speaking."

"This is Michael ...Williamson ...."

"*Michael!* Is it really? How wonderful! My goodness ...." she paused for a moment, "I hope nothing is wrong?"

"No, no. Everything is fine. Everything and everyone ... in fact, I just talked with my mother, who helped me find you. Everyone's great, even the dog.

"The reason I'm calling is because I'm in town. I'm up here working on a project and I remembered you live in San Francisco. I thought I'd visit you this weekend, if it's convenient ... if you want to."

"I'd love to see you, Michael. I'm just on my way to go shopping with a friend, but I can use you as a reason to escape. I always spend too much money when I go shopping with her. Let's meet for lunch."

Michael agreed and she named a time and a place.

Several hours later, as Michael walked into the unfamiliar restaurant, his eyes adjusting to the darkness, he realized that it had been fifteen years since he'd seen his aunt, and she could be considerably changed. He, of course, had been a child when she'd last seen him, so he definitely looked entirely different.

As the *maitre'd* walked up to him, he noticed a beautiful brunette woman straight in front of him who looked exactly as he'd remembered Aunt Alison when he was a boy. But of course, this woman could not be her, she was far too young. And, yet, after he'd given Aunt Alison's name to the *maitre'd*, he was led straight to the beautiful woman's table.

"Aunt Alison?" Michael asked.

"So it *is* you," she replied. "Please sit. When you walked in the door, you fairly took my breath away, you look so much like Anthony when he was your age."

Michael smiled. "When *I* came through the door, I thought you looked like you, but I told myself that this woman is entirely too young to be Aunt Alison. I mean, I hate to discuss a lady's age, but you have not changed one bit since I the last time I saw you when I was a child."

"Thank you, Michael, you're so charming."

"Not a bit. I'm entirely serious...."

The waiter came up. Michael took a moment to look at the menu and then ordered.

"Tell me more about yourself and your family," Alison asked enthusiastically. "What you're doing here, so forth and so on, all the details!"

"I have a job designing computer chips in Orange County ...."

"Did your uncle arrange that?"

"As a matter of fact, yes. And that's why I'm up in this territory, I'm trying to iron out some problems with a chip that's in production. Then, like I said, I remembered that you live here."

"Yes."

"I can't get over how you haven't changed!"

Alison smiled. "That's so sweet. But, to tell the truth, I've changed considerably. I'm independent, I'm much stronger. And … I *like* myself."

"Of course you like yourself. How could you not like yourself? *Everyone* likes you."

"Everyone *else* liked me because I was sweet and utterly agreeable. But I did not like *myself* that way. Now I'm strong, and that's the way I like it. But enough about me, I want to hear more about you!"

"No, it's *not* enough about you. I want you to tell me everything about yourself too," Michael insisted. "I tried to look you up, but the only Alison Williamson that came up was an artist who's apparently fairly famous. Lots of gallery shows and the like."

Alison giggled shyly. "Well, Michael, I'm … I have to tell you that that's … me."

"No!" Michael said, pleased and surprised, all at once.

"Yes. I left Orange County after getting a small show up here, and, well, things have really taken off. I've been blessed to have people love my work, and I appear to have a talent teaching."

"I couldn't be happier to hear it, Aunt Alison."

"Yes, my life has focus and meaning. After that first little show, I went to art school, studied with a couple of amazing teachers who pulled my muse out from her recesses. And I've been creating non-stop since.

"Nothing like great teachers to make a woman realize she's got talent," she affirmed.

"*If* she does," Michael mused.

"Everyone has a talent, or a skill or a desire. But some people need events in their lives that force them to get at it and either work at what they know about themselves, or find out what they *don't* know."

Michael nodded, appreciating her philosophy. "You must show me some of your work."

"I thought you'd never ask!" she answered, with a twinkle. "If you're free, we can go now. And I won't have to fight all these spoils of shopping in and out of taxis." She gestured to the pile of shiny department store bags by her side.

"Let's go!" Michael leapt up and gathered her booty, then led Alison to his rental car.

Alison directed him to a small but charming Victorian house in the Nob Hill district.

"Just put the things down anywhere, I'll deal with them later," she said when they came in.

"Nice place, Aunt Alison." Michael looked around at a wonderland of art from floor to ceiling as he carefully placed all the packages he'd carried in for her in the entryway, in the light of the cheerful stained glass window.

"Thank you, Michael." She hung her wrap in the hall closet. "Let's see, I'll give you a mini tour."

She took him on a tour of the little house, including the charming box of a back yard where a riot of colorful flowers grew in flower boxes.

"I love flowers," she said. "I like vegetables, and of course, they're more practical. I grow a few tomatoes and cucumbers, but I really love to grow colorful, fragrant flowers."

When they returned to the drawing room, the late afternoon light cut an angle through the bay window that faced the bay. All the walls were covered in original art by famous, or eventually-to-be famous, or never-to-be famous artists. Michael wandered about, drinking it all in, nearly overwhelmed.

"My taste is pretty eclectic, as you can see."

"But where's *your* work, Aunt Alison? I don't see your signature on anything."

Alison pointed to a stand with a portfolio on it. "I've some things in there. I always think I'm going to put up something of my own. I always think that the work in progress will be the one I'll feel like putting on my wall. But by the time it's done, I'm working on the next one in my mind, and the previous one pales. On and on it goes like that. Meanwhile, I'll go to a show, see something by an artist that I think is spectacular, and that's what ends up on my walls. I'm a funny old lady, aren't I?"

"No. At least, you're not old, but you *are* amusing."

Thumbing through the portfolio, Michael stopped short on a pencil sketch of what surely had to be Sage as a child, holding hands with Anthony. Michael pulled it out. "Is this ....?"

"Sage and Anthony. Do you know Sage?"

"As it happens, yes, I've met her."

"She must have been about nine there. She came and stayed with her aunt for a couple of weeks that summer. Who could know the tragedy the near future held for that dear child? Less than three years after that drawing her parents died in a plane crash."

"Yes, I know," Michael answered quietly.

"How is she?"

"What little I know of her, she's ... okay. I don't know how much you keep up with what goes on with those people ...."

"Frankly, Michael, I avoid it."

Michael suddenly realized that his presence might pain his aunt. "I didn't think ... does my being here ... are you uncomfortable?"

"Do I seem uncomfortable? No, my dear, I'm very, very happy to see you, and that you looked me up, and that you're here. Don't take my meaning wrong. There's only one person that I don't want to encounter personally ... or even mentally."

"Oh. Uncle Anthony, I suppose."

"No, not your Uncle Anthony. Sage's Aunt Victoria."

"Really? How strange, I was just going to tell you, I guess you don't know ... I was just going to tell you that she died fairly recently."

Aunt Alison, who had been standing by Michael moved to the love seat, slightly pale.

"Are you okay?" Michael came over to her, concerned.

"I'm fine ... I ... I'm fine. It's just that when you know you've wished someone no good in your heart, and then you hear they've died, it's startling. Be careful what you wish, dear nephew of mine, it may surprise you by becoming fulfilled."

"I hope you don't mind my asking, Aunt Alison, but I've gotten this feeling that there was something uniquely bad about Sage's aunt from everyone but Sage. She's devoted to her."

"There are two things I can say about Sage's devotion to her aunt, one, that that devotion is central to Sage's character. She's very true. I noticed that about her even when she was a child. Her loyalties are inflexible. And two, I am quite certain she doesn't know everything there is to know about her aunt."

"Well, my curiosity is about as piqued as it can get," Michael said. "Would you mind filling me in?"

"No, Michael, I don't mind. I think the time has come. Sage's Aunt Victoria is, I guess I should say *was* an exceptionally bright and beautiful woman. But she always had a plan in mind. You had the feeling around her that she was weighing and measuring every situation, every person.

"She could never to go a party and just have fun, or just get to know people because they were interesting. She socialized in order to size people up, to dissect their inter-personal relationships, to see where she could finagle her way in and get ... whatever it was she wanted. More property, more money, more things.

"Her poor husband. We were always so mystified how he managed to get rich in the *first* place, let alone keep his hands on it. He was, candidly, not particularly bright. However, as long as he was alive, things were all right. But the moment he died, Victoria really went into action. And her target was my husband."

"Uncle Anthony?"

"Yes. I watched him go from hating her, which he did when Evan first married her and brought her to that hill, to admiring and believing the act she put on when Evan died. As if she were stricken with grief and as if she could barely endure the loss. Then I watched as he became entangled with her."

Michael studied his aunt, sitting in the fading rays of the bay window sun, looking over her shoulder through the window. He could feel her pain, remembering these events, and he could feel her strength in having learned to live with the memories.

She continued, "She'd call him at all hours to go to her place and do anything from check a legal document to repair a fence. Or for other who-konws-what reasons. I knew it immediately. Anthony is not a man who can divide his loyalties. Once she sank her claws into him, he was lost.

"To this day I don't know how I endured that awful situation as long as I did. I stuck it out for a couple of years, everything in limbo. Anthony refusing to give in to Victoria entirely, that is, he wouldn't divorce me. Victoria, not letting him go. And me, not doing anything either. Just—in limbo. Hoping, I suppose, he'd either come out from under her spell, or that she'd get bored and find someone else.

"I've realized since then that it was really a contest—for her—against *me*. She didn't care about Anthony other than that he was rich and good-looking. But her real emotions were stirred up in her efforts to win Anthony over me.

"In the end, I was the one who showed the real strength. Anyone would say that it was Anthony or Victoria who are the strong characters and I'm the weak one, but I was the one who said, enough, I won't have this anymore. I finally refused to accept only a part of my husband, and I refused to be any part of Victoria's psychological bizarreness to prove herself the most desirable woman.

"I woke up at four a.m. one morning and thought, 'I'm not going to do this any more. It's humiliating and it's consuming me.' I got out of bed, packed a few things, flew here and filed for divorce.

"Well, it seems that Victoria didn't find that particularly interesting, because, as my grapevine that I was still somewhat hooked up to back then informed me, as soon as I left, she cooled toward Anthony."

Michael moved to sit in the chair by Alison's love seat. "He became available, so why bother?"

"Exactly."

"But why didn't Uncle Anthony try to get you back? He must have seen Victoria for what she was."

"I don't know, Michael, except what I *do* know of him, he's a person who, once he feels humiliated, and is not sure of the territory, does not want to discover that he's making a further nincompoop of himself. I, of course, was not about to go back to him and get Victoria started all over again."

"How strange," Michael said.

"Yes. Life is often strange," Alison agreed. She sighed, then turned to Michael. "But tell me about Sage. Is she as beautiful a woman as she was a child? What kind of a person is she, with Victoria's influence, did she stay sweet, or did she turn into someone less pleasant?"

"She's an incredibly beautiful woman, Aunt Alison ... remarkable. And, although I've had little interaction with her, she seems to me to be as sincere, honest and straight forward a person as anyone would hope to meet in life."

Michael wondered if he ought to mention what appeared to be a possible relationship between Sage and Anthony, but decided to keep it to himself. He wasn't certain of it, and, given what his aunt thought of Sage, it almost certainly would cause unnecessary pain.

Alison stood and moved about the drawing room, turning on Victorian lamps with mellow flickering lights, as evening shadows stole into the corners of the room. "It sounds," she said in her gentle voice, "as though you care for her in a personal way."

"It does?"

"Yes. Not so much in the words you're using as in the quality of your voice."

"Never mind me," Michael said off-handedly. "I can't be held responsible when I talk about women, I've been trapped in a chip production lab for so long, any talk about real people is likely to sound strange."

His aunt studied him for a long moment until he became uncomfortable. Okay, he wanted to say, you've caught me in a white lie, but I'm between a rock and a hard place.

"So what about you?" he said instead. "I mean, what about you *now*? How do you feel about Uncle Anthony now?"

"Getting personal back at me, eh? I care about him, of course. I've dated a lot, probably more than Anthony, but I've never fallen in love again. There's nothing like that first love. I believe people look all their lives for it if they lose it. But even if a person looks forever for someone to replace that love, only first love is first love. I sometimes find myself thinking that Anthony and I should never have been apart. But what is, *is*. You can't undo it."

"Maybe one can start over," Michael suggested.

Alison came and sat on the arm of Michael's chair and put her arm around him. "For a computer nerd you're pretty romantic."

"There's a bumper sticker in there somewhere— 'computer nerds are romantics too.' Or maybe I'm not really a computer nerd."

Chapter 15
Sage

Tina met Sage outside the social science building after their evening class.

"How are all your ologies?"

"Excuse me?"

"Archeology, anthropology—ologies."

Sage chuckled. "My ologies are great. I love them."

"That's good. You wanna go out and play?"

They came to Sage's new car. "I've got to get straight home and study, although I'm so tired, I don't even feel like driving. Of course, in my zippy, new, little red car it's a lot more fun than in the whale."

"But think of all the attention you're missing that you used to get when you drove the limo!"

"Yet another plus now. Traveling incognito."

"Oh, yeah, I remember the motorcycle gang," Tina said, getting into Sage's car.

"Awful," Sage said, recalling that evening. Remembering Michael. That night, seeming now *sooo* long ago and far away. Her life had changed dramatically since then.

She pulled up to Tina's apartment. "I'll pick you up Thursday, six-thirty, sharp!"

"Okay!" Tina gathered her books and bag and got out. "Don't study too hard."

"Don't know any other way," Sage answered, waving as she pulled away.

Michael.

It wasn't as if she'd not thought of him recently. She thought of him every day. Then quickly pushed her mind to other thoughts. But she hadn't thought of that first time she saw him in some while.

Ever since she'd gotten back from Jamaica over a month ago, Dahlia's chat stuck in her mind. But she couldn't figure out how to make a move on it. Everything around her seemed contrived to make her think about Michael, while at the same time, everything contrived not to let her see him or talk with him.

She saw Millie a couple of days a week, she frequently talked with or went over to Anthony's. Michael was mentioned casually in passing by both. But he was never around. She knew he'd gone to San Francisco on business right after she got back from Jamaica. But she didn't know if he was there, or if he'd returned.

She gave it up to the *Powers* that oversee such things and threw herself into her studies.

Fortunately, she loved studying.

*   *

Thursday night after class, Tina ran up to Sage's car, breathless and all aglow. "I don't need a ride home tonight, I'm going to do my cooking class homework with John."

"I know you thought I'd never ask, but who's John?" Sage shifted her pile of books from the crook of one arm to the other.

"He's a chef ... in my cooking class. He's incredible!" Tina gushed.

"A chef in a first year cooking class?"

"He has to have the credits for a new job he just got. Oh, Sage! This time it's really something. I can just tell—as long as I don't blow it. He said he noticed me the first night of class. He said my hair is very sensual. He said that chefs are sensually oriented. He said that it's his belief that anyone with a heightened sense of taste has heightened other senses as well.

"Then he said ... and you know a guy doesn't say this if he's just coming on, he said that although he loved my hair, he only 'likes' my face and body. He said I'll be perfect when he's managed to put a few pounds on me!"

Sage gave her friend a hug. "Have fun. Call me tomorrow and let me know how it all went."

"I will!"

Tina didn't call for two days, and when she did, she sounded lethargic and far away. "John and I have been working on some of those Cajun recipes I brought back from Jamaica. I'm in a stupor."

Sage tried to envision her friend chubby.

"And in love?" she asked.

"Yes, we're in a complete wallow of stuporous exotic food and love."

"*Stop!*" Sage protested, laughing. "I can only take so much. Remember, I'm your spinster friend."

"I'm so happy."

"And I'm happy you're happy."

Tina giggled. "Johnny's tickling me. Okay, back to work. I'll call you, Sage."

"I won't hold my breath. But please do send me a wedding invitation."

"You know I will!"

After Sage hung up, she wondered if she wasn't just a tad envious. She felt truly happy for her friend, but she also suddenly felt empty and lonely.

"Get back to your studying," she reminded herself.

And so for the rest of the weekend, she kept occupied with her "ologies" and gardening.

Monday morning as she looked over her calendar, she noticed Anthony's birthday was only three weeks away. It would be a pleasant diversion to plan a party for him, not to mention how much he deserved it considering how selflessly he'd given of himself and his resources of late.

She'd give an elegant party near the ocean, for the people closest to him. The Ritz-Carlton would be perfect.

The three of them, Anthony, Aunt Victoria, and she, used to go there for dinner or to listen to the chamber music, sipping a beverage, watching the ocean. She knew Anthony loved the Ritz-Carlton. She spent the morning making out a tentative guest list and menu.

She thought perhaps Tina and John might like to help. Maybe, if they helped cater the party, they could get some college credit.

She then called a small handful of the people on her guest list to ask their opinions of her party plans. She had to leave messages for the first two people she called. But the dowager princess was always home, unless she was abroad or at a party. She loved every bit of Sage's party plan and said she'd help in any way, from cooking to bringing her portable disc-jockey studio.

Reassured by the dowager's enthusiasm, Sage screwed up her courage and dialed the number she had for Michael. Her dreams of him had subsided some, although not entirely. And, of course, Dahlia's serious proclamation never seemed to lose its intensity. But she became even more un-nerved when the phone was answered by the Micro Silicon company switchboard. She didn't realize that the only number she had for Michael was his work number. After asking for him by name, a phone rang several times, then she heard Michael's abstracted hello.

"Hello, Michael, this is Sage Elgin. Sorry to bother you at work. I didn't realize that the only number I have for you is your work number."

"Yes?"

Even more non-plussed by his coolness, she plunged on. "I'm planning a birthday party for Anthony three weeks from Friday at, I thought, the Ritz-Carlton. I'm just calling a few of the people on my tentative guest list to see how that suits everyone."

"Sounds fine, Sage, but why are you asking me? I don't even know the Ritz-Carlton."

"Oh ... I didn't realize. I thought the Ritz-Carlton would be nice because it's on the ocean, and has excellent facilities. I don't feel up to having it at my place since I have no staff. And I'm asking you, as you're his closest relative. I want to make sure the date doesn't conflict with your schedule."

"It sounds fine to me, Sage. It's a thoughtful thing for you to do."

"So you'll be there?"

There was a long, and to Sage, a peculiar silence from the other end.

"I ought to, oughtn't I? I've no schedule conflict. But I have to say Sage, that I feel ... I feel I have to talk with you about something beforehand."

Now it was Sage's turn for the long, silent pause. "Of course, Michael. Anytime. Can you give me a clue as to the subject?"

"It's ... it's complicated. In fact, I need some time to think it through. It's Monday, how about Wednesday evening?"

"Okay. I have a class from seven to nine, shall I meet you somewhere in your neck of the woods after class?"

"That'd be convenient ... I usually get home from work around seven or seven-thirty. Perhaps you wouldn't mind coming to my condo."

"Okay."

Michael gave her his address and cell phone number. Sage was left to puzzle for two days what he could possibly have to talk with her about.

*   *

Sage could hardly pay the least bit of attention in class on Wednesday night, and now she stood at Michael's door, pressing the doorbell, curious and nervous.

"Hi," he said, ushering her in. "How are you?"

"I'm fine."

"You look great," they both said at the same moment, then laughed, somewhat uncomfortably.

"Well, you do look great!" Michael insisted. "Would you care for anything?"

"I'd love a glass of water. I always feel dehydrated after a couple classes."

"Water coming right up. Please, make yourself comfortable." Michael gestured to the sofa.

Sage took in the room as she moved to the sofa. Nice. Clean. A bit spartan, but a couple of elegant paintings on the wall. Nice furniture.

Michael returned and handed her a tall glass of ice water.

"What class were you in this evening?" He asked politely, but not sitting. His hovering made Sage yet more nervous.

"My worst ... statistics."

"Statistics! What's your major?"

"Anthropology. I ... my father was an anthro-pologist. Anyway, I don't want to get into my personal ... ahm ... not when you have an urgent subject. What is it you wanted to talk with me about?"

Sage turned her huge blue eyes up to him.

"Yes ... well, ah ..." Michael paced to the patio sliding door, looked out at the dark yard. "Ah ... boy, I'm having more trouble with this than I expected. It suddenly seems to me I should keep my mouth shut. I dislike meddlers and I'm beginning to feel like one."

Sage said nothing, closely watching his discomfort, entirely mystified.

"I design computer chips ...."

"Yes?"

"A few weeks ago I got sent up north to work on one that's in production. So I was near San Francisco. Do you remember my Aunt Alison?"

Confused, Sage's brow furrowed. "Yes, Michael, I do, with great affection."

"Yes. Good. Me too. With affection. So I ... I looked her up."

"Wonderful! How is she?"

"She's well. Beautiful, hasn't aged a bit. I mean, she really hasn't aged one bit! And sweeter than ever. She's become an artist of notable repute, and showed me some of her remarkable work. I really like it. I guess that's what everyone always says about art ... 'I know what I like.' I got these from her."

He gestured to the two graphics that had taken Sage's attention. "I keep trying to pay her for them, but she keeps returning my VISA transactions."

Sage gave the graphics more study. "They're wonderful, Michael. Goodness, I didn't know this about her. Quite a talent. Thank you for sharing this with me," Sage said, friendly, yet more mystified.

"That's not all, though. I was thumbing through a portfolio she had and there was a pencil sketch of you and Uncle Anthony. She had wonderful things to say about you, by the way."

"Did she? The last time I saw her, I was only a child, but she had a huge influence on me. More than, I suppose, she even realizes."

"She feels you're very special and was happy to hear that you're doing well. But then our conversation turned to your Aunt Victoria."

"Oh?" Sage didn't care for the subtle change in the tone of Michael's voice.

"Aunt Alison didn't know about what happened ...." Michael went on.

"Really? That's surprising. She must still have some friends in common, or read the paper."

"Whatever the case may be, she didn't know. Anyway, the subject of your Aunt Victoria brought up some interesting information."

"What do you mean?"

"I wish I understood why I feel so compelled to tell you about this. In part I seem to need to make amends to my Aunt Alison. Which is ridiculous because these are events that happened when I was a child and I lived thousands of miles from here. I couldn't be less involved. And you were a child too. I'm assuming you knew nothing ...."

"Please, Michael," Sage interrupted, becoming agitated, "get to the point, or to *some* point!"

"Yes, the point, which is, that after your Aunt Victoria's husband died, she engaged in a flirtation with my Uncle Anthony, until she succeeded in drawing him away from his marriage, which eventually led to my Aunt Alison leaving him."

Sage felt her temper rise. She stood up. "Why *is* it everyone feels the compulsion to attack my Aunt Victoria? Whatever happened to the notion of not speaking ill of the dead? She's not here to defend herself. She was a strong woman. People always seem to hate strong women, I've noticed. And you, Michael, we're not personal friends, but you've seen the effect castigating my aunt can have on me. *Why* would you communicate Alison's imagined wrongs to me?"

Michael came over to Sage and pulled her down on the sofa beside him.

"Please, Sage, relax." Consternation on his face and in his voice. "I told you, I hate this sort of involvement. I avoid it like a plague. But, for this particular set of circumstances, I'm positive Aunt Alison is not fabricating. You and my uncle obviously have a commitment to one another. It's completely none of my business, but I come to you because you and I are the people who care about the people involved."

"First of all, I am *not* involved with your uncle, other than as a dear friend. Secondly, what do you want me to do, Michael?" Sage tried hard to be calm and polite, but this was *so* unexpected.

"I honestly don't know. Since I saw Aunt Alison, I've been at my wits end. I didn't know how I'd behave, or what I'd say when next I saw you. Then you called. So I've just talked. But, in addition to my concern for my Uncle Anthony and Aunt Alison, wouldn't you be upset if you … moved forward into a relationship and sometime later found out he'd had an affair with your aunt, and that it was the cause of his divorce?"

"It's Just. Not. True." Sage breathed deeply. "You don't strike me as the type to be a gossip-monger, but I've been wrong before. Further, you're not only demeaning my aunt, who cannot defend herself, but you're saying awful things about your own uncle."

"I know. I know. That's why—it's *all* why I haven't talked with you. I didn't want to know what I now know. But, what if Alison still loves Anthony? What if …."

"I think this whole notion is a fabrication of Alison's," Sage interrupted. "I like her too, Michael, and I don't like to speak badly of her, but it sounds like a lonely woman's unchecked imagination."

"She's hardly lonely. Her life is full and busy. She has gallery shows, she teaches art. She doesn't need to fabricate anything. And why would she leave Uncle Anthony in the first place? Why would he let her leave?"

"I don't know, Michael. I've never pried into Anthony's personal life. What he chooses to tell me, fine. What he does not choose to tell me, also fine. Why don't you ask *him*?"

Sage stood up again, somewhat more calm and collected. "He's my friend. Friends have the right to share what they want to share and to withhold what they consider private. I have boundless respect for Anthony."

"I know, Sage. I do too."

"He's been a wonderful, dependable friend. Now I'd like to thank him in small measure by giving him a little birthday party. I'm hoping you'll come. You're absence would be utterly conspicuous, and would hurt Anthony."

"You're right, Sage. I'll be at the party, of course. Please let me know if there's anything I can do to help. Regarding the past, I will respect your opinion and let it rest."

Michael walked Sage to the door, where they parted amiably. But each wondered why they felt so miserable.

Chapter 16
Sage

Sage was glad for the long drive home after she left Michael's condo. She wanted to think and think and *think*—and driving let her do it.

Why would Alison want to tell Michael this story? She *must* believe it was true. Could she possibly be the type of person who made things up to suit herself? But she'd never behaved like that in all of Sage's limited experience with her. It simply didn't ring true.

And why, why, *why* did Michael insist on giving her this information? It made her incredibly unhappy. It made her upset with Michael, it made her upset with Anthony, it made her upset with Alison. And, she was surprised to discover, it made her upset with Aunt Victoria.

Michael was not a malicious person. He hadn't told her to give her pain, and it had been clear it was hard for him to have this talk with her. She replayed the tension she saw in him as he stood at his patio door, his back to her, but his face reflected darkly in the glass. He'd looked as though he would prefer to melt right through the glass rather than share with her what his Aunt Alison had told him.

He'd told her, of course, out of some sense of duty or obligation, some belief that it was the right thing to do. But she couldn't understand why just leaving it alone would not have been a better choice.

Then she realized, without a doubt, Michael had gone through these same thoughts. He was trying to tell her to get out of the way, to give Anthony and Alison another chance. He'd almost said as much. Of course, as she understood him, it would be impossible for Michael to tell her to leave his uncle alone if he believed there was something between them.

But there wasn't.

It would not be difficult to remove herself entirely from Anthony's life. But the hard part was believing Aunt Victoria would intentionally break up a marriage.

When she got home, she poured herself a glass of wine and went into her aunt's office. There was a small, two-drawer wooden file cabinet that she'd peeked into once. She'd seen it was personal memorabilia and diaries, and she'd closed the drawer, wondering if she'd ever have the courage to peer into it again.

The moment had arrived.

She pulled a few of the file folders out, and arrayed them on the oriental carpet. Then she sat on the floor, took a long deep drink of wine and opened the first folder. It was more or less chronological, from the most recent backwards. There were stacks of letters to and from people Sage had never heard of. Photographs of attractive men on yachts, on horseback, on impeccably manicured golf courses. Aunt Victoria was in some of the pictures, generally smiling seriously at either the photographer, whoever that might be, or smiling seriously at the various men she stood next to.

In one unopened letter, Sage hesitated, but finally opened it and found an unused round trip ticket to London, dated ten years previous, from a man that her aunt had apparently so completely lost interest in, she hadn't even bothered to open his letter.

Sage felt sorry for this anonymous man whose signature she couldn't read, whose heartfelt emotions on the page, what little Sage could make out, were school boyish and pathetically sincere. Sage knew such a man would never stand a chance with her aunt. It didn't matter how rich he may be, he'd have to be tougher and harder to get and keep her interest.

She remembered how Aunt Victoria had always teased her whenever she behaved kindly toward someone. She wanted Sage to be tough.

She continued to thumb through the pile of photographs she'd never seen before. Everyone always seemed to recede when near her Aunt Vicky. Sage remembered her image of herself as a light shadow trapped in the penumbra of her aunt's world.

But there was not one piece of incriminating evidence to support Michael's—or Alison's—premise. Not one note, not one picture, from or to or about Anthony. It appeared just as Sage believed. That the only time Victoria socialized with Anthony, Sage was with them. The three of them always did everything together after her aunt's husband died. It was the same both before and after Alison left.

Feeling relieved yet confused, Sage put the letters and photos back in the drawer and went upstairs to bed.

But as she came to the head of the stairs, she found herself drawn to Aunt Vicky's room instead of her own. She opened the massive walnut door and crept in. She'd never been in this room at night since her childhood. She turned on all the lights. Why couldn't she get the notion of her aunt still inhabiting this room out of her head, her heart? Some day she'd have to go through everything.

But for the moment, she was trying to maintain her peace of mind. Where to begin? The room was full of closets and dressers. She cautiously opened a few drawers.

Aunt Victoria's distinctive, expensive, and notable perfumes poured over Sage like rain. All of the feelings of loss she'd been trying to keep under control pounded on her until she felt she'd burst. But, for once, she would be tough like her aunt always wanted.

She began cautiously, running her slender hands in and around the scented lingerie and sweaters. Aunt Vicky is gone, Sage told herself, she'd never come back and interrogate her about why she'd gone through her personal things, or why the perfectly folded clothes were rumpled.

Sage felt an anger mounting toward her aunt. Why did she have to make people hate her so much that they wished her dead, like Bill Rattnor had? Sage had never heard *anyone* say they liked Victoria, much less loved her.

Then Sage remembered what Rattnor had said in his rantings, all of which she'd dismissed as insanity, that awful day in court. He'd said that Victoria had teased him, and after her husband died, she'd become involved in Anthony. Sage remembered now the look Rattnor had given Anthony when he began this harangue. She'd not had the courage to look at Anthony in that moment.

She began to throw things from drawers, no longer any regard for their carefully folded placement. She thought about the change in Anthony's character since her aunt died. Before he seemed always on edge. Even, sometimes, a bit mean.

Was it possible that after Alison left, if, indeed, Aunt Victoria had intended to break up that marriage, that she wasn't interested in what was then accessible? It would be like her to no longer want Anthony, but she *would* consider it expedient to keep him and all his wealth in the family by having him marry Sage.

Sage came upon a purple crushed velvet box with a small gold lock. She tried picking at the lock with a safety pin, but losing patience, she ripped at the lock until it broke open. This behavior was so unlike her, she felt, for a minute, inhabited by her aunt's personality.

In the purple crushed velvet box lay everything she hoped she would not find. A few affectionate letters from Anthony dated prior to his divorce, pictures of Aunt Victoria and Anthony together—without Sage. All those times Aunt Vicky had said she had to leave on business, she'd been with Anthony.

Here it lay, carefully and unmistakably documented. Unlike the pictures downstairs of the nondescript men, these were pictures of two strong, attractive, powerful people. Her aunt did not over-shadow Anthony.

But after Alison left Anthony, there were only a couple more letters from him to Victoria, and gradually their expression changed. There were only a couple pictures of them together, with an obvious emotional distance between them.

Sage sat on the floor in the middle of clothing and pictures strewn around her. The letters from Anthony made it clear of her aunt's motivation. His letters began with defending his loyalty to Alison, and, although he found Victoria attractive, he begged her to respect his marriage and not try to interfere. Then the letters expressed a more confused state of loyalties, until finally he declared he'd do anything to make Victoria happy, now that Alison was gone.

Then there were no more letters. She recalled what Tina had said about her "readings" of Anthony. That there was some sort of tinge upon him.

And here it was.

Sage couldn't get angry, she couldn't cry. She stood up, left everything just as it was and took herself to bed.

*　　*

When Sage woke the next morning, she realized that now it was *her* turn to practice what she preached. She would not speak ill of the dead, nor, for that matter, the living. She felt liberated. Aunt Victoria had been, after all, just a person. At times, not a nice person. Not a nice person at all.

Sage realized she could finally let her go. And she could let Anthony go as well. He was a dear sweet man who wanted, and who deserved, to be loved. She began to devise a plan that, one way or another, she'd persuade Alison to come to Anthony's birthday party.

Not only that, but somehow she'd apologize to Michael. It had taken real bravery for him to tell her what Alison told him, but he'd done it out of love for the people involved.

As she thought about it, Sage admitted to herself that she loved Michael, too. She'd loved him from the first moment she saw him when he unwittingly rescued her from the motorcyclists, to this very moment when she realized he would sacrifice his own pride to let truth reign, and in an effort to make those he cared about happy.

What had she been doing all these months, marking time, thinking about him from afar? She didn't have to wonder if he cared about her, she knew. She knew, even if he didn't.

She got up, got dressed, went downstairs, made a pot of tea, and called Anthony.

"You busy?"

"Never too busy for you, Sage."

"I need to chat with you. I'll be over in a few minutes."

Anthony, himself, answered the door, and led her into his office. "I hope this is not another visit prompted by trauma?...." he asked hesitatingly.

Sage smiled. "No, Anthony, not at all! I want to make sure that the guest of honor comes to his own party."

"What?"

"I'm planning a birthday party for you. I've called a few people, they're all set to have a gala event at the Ritz-Carlton the day after your birthday, on the Friday."

Anthony smiled boyishly. "Sage, you shouldn't!"

"I *should* and I want to. I need something concrete to put my mind on. I've only been planning this party for a couple of days and it's been a lot of fun already. All I need from you is for you to say you'll be there."

"I'll be there! This is amazing. No one has given me a birthday party since ... well, in years."

"Since Alison, isn't that true?"

Anthony's expression sobered. "Yes, since Alison. And now you, Sage, you give me this honor."

"You deserve it, Anthony. By the way, did you know that Michael recently saw Alison?"

"Really? No, I didn't. I haven't seen him in weeks."

"He happened to mention it when I invited him to your party."

"How is she?"

"He said she's doing well. I guess she's an established artist, and is pretty successful."

"Yes," Anthony said, "I know about her art, a little."

"Do you ever think about her?" Sage asked.

"Of course I do, sometimes ... I mean, I remember, you know, our past, when we were young, when things were easier."

"Hmmm."

"Well, she was my first love. You know how bonding they say a first love is. I think it sets your tone of mind and heart for life. You remind me so much of Alison, your quiet yet strong character. Isn't it strange that you're more like Alison, than your own Aunt?"

"But Anthony," Sage pointed out, "if my character is as you say, and I hope it is, it stems from my parents. My father left this area, to be with my mother for the precise reason that he was drawn to her wise and quiet nature."

"That's true, that's true," Anthony became reflective.

"As a child, I role-modeled Alison. I loved my aunt, but I wanted to be like Alison."

"Yes? I'm glad to hear you say that." He returned his full attention to the moment. "But—a birthday party—for me! I'm not going to ask any questions, I'm just going to let everything be a surprise."

"That's a good birthday boy," Sage giggled. "I'll talk to you later. But right now I've got to get back to getting it organized."

At home Sage scrounged through her desk until she found a letter Alison had written her years ago when she first moved to San Francisco. In it she'd given Sage her phone number—"In case you ever need to talk with me."

That time had arrived. Sage dialed the number and, miraculously, Alison answered.

"Alison, this is Sage Elgin."

"Sage? Little Sage?" Alison's youthful voice sounded thrilled to hear Sage.

"Well," Sage laughed, "all-grown-up Sage. Michael mentioned he'd seen you recently. He had glowing things to say about you. I'm so glad Michael talked to you, reminding me how much I miss you."

"Oh, Sage!" There was a catch in Alison's voice, "you're going to make me cry!"

"Don't cry Alison. But ... I believe Michael mentioned to you the misfortune that befell my Aunt Vicky. And I ... I've come to realize how important people are to one another. And you, especially, to me, Alison. I really want to see you. And, what's more, I'm giving Anthony a birthday party the day after his birthday. Please come down and be my guest that weekend ...."

"Oh, I don't know, Sage, it sounds a little ...."

"It's *not*," Sage protested. "It's not a little sticky or whatever. I don't want to betray a confidence, but you should hear the way Anthony talks about you. The two of you should at least be friends. If anyone is fortunate enough to live long enough to bury the hatchet, to forgive and be forgiven, I think, I mean, I *believe* that that is one of life's greatest gifts.

"No one is perfect. We all make mistakes. But, at the same time, we all just want 'to love and to be loved' as the song says. So please come and be with us. It's not only about Anthony, it's about me, and about Michael, and about all your friends here who love you. Come down and be with us."

"Sage, you're irresistible. What a sweet girl. I mean, young woman! I have a picture of you in my mind's eye as a beautiful little girl."

"So you'll come? I can count on you?"

"I'll come. And Sage?" Alison paused. "Thank you."

Chapter 17
Sage & Michael

It was a fresh, breezy Indian summer day the day of Anthony's party. One of those days so rare in southern California, a New England-like day, when the air had summer warmth with an overlay of autumn bite. Sage loved a day such as this more than any other. It reminded her of her favorite days in her childhood, when she and her mother and father would roam the woods.

She picked up Alison at the John Wayne airport in the morning, the two of them delighted to see one another, with warm hugs.

"Michael was right. He insisted you haven't changed a bit, and it's so true. I knew you the instant I saw you."

"And you, my dear," Alison returned affectionately, what a statuesque beauty you've become!"

After their mutual adoration reacquaintance, Sage left Alison off at her home to rest and get ready for the party.

"Let me come with you to help set up the party," Alison said once again.

"No way, you are on a no-work-allowed holiday. Besides," Sage reminded her, "you're supposed to be a surprise for Anthony and everyone else, so you're not to show yourself until the party!"

At the Ritz-Carlton, Sage was greatly relieved to see Millie already there, buzzing about, taking care of details. Sage okayed flower and table arrangements, made sure the sound check was going well with the musicians and helped the dowager princess set up her intermission recorded music. She paused for a few moments, drinking in the on-the-ocean view from the glass-walled party room. Then she went to the small kitchen behind the party room.

There Tina and John were making dozens of hors d'oeuvres, dinner, and desserts that would be talked about in glowing terms for a long, long time to come.

Sage sampled the concoctions piling up in the small kitchen. "My goodness," she laughed, "there's only going to be forty or fifty guests. It looks like you're cooking for three hundred!"

"We've got freezers for extras," a harried and happy Tina said, dashing around Sage.

"You love this, don't you?"

Tina stopped to grin at Sage. "I *really* love this. I have a sense of purpose, and I'm doing something that makes people happy."

"You're making *me* extremely happy, that's for sure," Sage affirmed.

"And John ... isn't he wonderful?"

The two women stood and admired John as he wielded the Mix Master with professional aplomb. Skinny as a rail, he looked improbable as one of the potentially greatest chefs in the country.

"He's kind of skinny, but he *is* awfully cute!" Sage whispered to Tina.

"He's just perfect. And he thinks I'm *almost* perfect." Tina patted her filling-out thighs.

"I never thought I'd say this to anyone, but you honestly *do* look better with a few pounds added. Healthier. Color in your cheeks, sparkle in your eye. You're cuter with the curves. Of course some of your cuteness is how much you're in love."

"Yes. Love." Tina tossed her head. "Okay, enough praise for the moment. I've got to get back to my slavery or the boss-lady is goin' ta fire me!"

"That will not happen." Sage returned to the party room, satisfied with everything in order. She needed to hurry home and make *herself* presentable.

Alison must be napping Sage thought when she got home, the house, peacefully quiet.

She went to her room and laid out her new turquoise blue and corn-silk yellow print dress and yellow sandals. She showered and washed her long hair, braided a few thin braids and wove blue corn flowers in among the braids. As she slipped on the dress, there was a knock at the door.

"Sage?"

"Come in, Alison."

Alison opened the door. "Oh, how lovely you look."

"Wow, Alison, look at you!"

Alison stood in the doorway in a jade green, tea-length, fitted silk sheath. "You're stunning! You'll take Anthony's breath away."

"You're too kind, sweetie. But I need to tell you that I'm feeling extremely nervous and having serious second thoughts. I really think I should not go."

"Nonsense," Sage led Alison to the love seat and sat beside her. "Quite frankly, I'm nervous too. I'm giving a party for some of the world's most sophisticated party goers. What if I've done some unwitting but awful *faux pas*?"

"Oh no, Sage. Everyone loves you. They just want to go to Anthony's party, they're not interested in trying to find fault."

Sage nodded, relieved. Alison was one-hundred percent right. She gave her a gentle, non-wrinkling, non mussing, but sincere, hug. "Thank you. You've always said the right thing to make everyone feel comfortable. Well, then," Sage stood, "nerves and all, do you suppose we can fool them into thinking we're cool as cucumbers?"

"We always do!"

They got into Sage's little car and raced down the canyon to the Ritz-Carlton, arriving half-an-hour before Anthony was to come.

After getting Alison comfortably settled in a near-by powder room, Sage went to the party room. All the musicians were there and on her cue they played soft classical music as the guests began to arrive.

She greeted everyone as they entered, feeling sure and unsure at the same moment. She'd never hosted a party before, although she had helped her aunt extensively many times. But this time the guests were saying that *she'd* done a lovely job with the room, that *she'd* gotten an excellent band, and where did she *find* the caterers who made these wonderful canapes?

She was so grateful to see Millie bustling about in the background, answering questions and being, as she'd become, her effective right hand.

Sage couldn't help watching for Michael, but he didn't come through the door. Disappointment mounted. She tried to set it aside, but she could not. She chided herself for not calling him to apologize, but she'd built up a fantasy about the happy surprise his Aunt Alison being at the party would be for him.

She'd intended to make her heartfelt apology to him tonight—to tell him he'd been completely right. And to thank him for making things better for everyone with his bravery.

But if he didn't come....

Right at that moment the guest of honor arrived, smiling like a little boy.

Anthony embraced Sage, and whispered in her ear, "I'd like to say a few words to everyone."

"Certainly!" She escorted him to the dais where the band played, then tapped on a wine glass to get everyone's attention.

"Dear friends," Anthony began, clearly touched by the warmth surrounding him, "I'm so honored tonight by all of you, my treasured friends. Sage, our hostess, deserves every accolade for this lovely event. Where Sage is, there too is charm and grace. Her equal would be hard to find!"

Sage stepped back, trying to get out of the limelight. "Please, Anthony, tonight is about *you*." She raised her glass.

Everyone raised a glass. "*Yes! Anthony!*" they chorused.

At that moment, Sage saw Michael enter, looking stormy and quite as though he'd rather not be here. She watched Millie hurry up to him, beaming at his arrival. His stormy visage turned to smiles as Millie gave him a hug.

Anthony continued, "This is the best birthday in my life, and I've had quite a few, so I know what I'm taking about!"

Everyone chuckled. Sage nodded at Millie, and Millie excused herself from Michael.

As Anthony continued with a few more niceties, a ripple of whispers ran through the crowd. Then Sage heard Anthony gasp as Alison stepped out from the crowd across from him. The last red rays of the setting sun outlined Alison's trim and goddess-like figure with an almost supernatural glow, while the green silk of her sheath reflected a golden sheen.

She was glorious.

Sage felt more than she saw the look Michael shot toward her when he turned from drinking in the stunning appearance of his aunt to his surprised admiration of Sage.

Anthony stepped down from the dais. *"Alison!"* He hurried up to her and took her hands in his.

"How are you Anthony?" she asked, cool as jade.

Anthony kissed her hands gallantly. "I'm fine. I'm more than fine—especially at the sight of you."

Anthony looked back at Sage. "You arranged this?"

"I did. And now everyone, let's party!" Sage urged.

The guests immediately responded to her command. They partied and ate and danced and chatted. Tina and John brought out delicacy after delicacy. Millie took care of all the little details like a pro.

Sage studied the overall effect. Everything was perfect. Everyone was happy.

She stepped outside and wandered among the giant columns, trying to understand the hole in her heart. She ought to be overflowing with happiness. It was odd how a person could make so many people happy, and herself be filled with sadness.

She leaned against one of the stark white pillars, studying the ocean, its white crests turning up in the moonlight, eternally coming into shore. Not happy, not sad—simply fulfilling its nature, washing to shore and being pulled back out to the ocean. Why couldn't she be like that? Just fulfill her calling, and not succumb to emotions that didn't help anything in any way.

"You've created a remarkable event," someone softly whispered nearby. Sage turned. Michael stood beside her, watching the ocean, too.

"Thank you, Michael. But it's the people who are here who have made a remarkable event. All I did was invite them." She turned to face his profile. "I owe you a profound apology. I went through my aunt's personal things that I never had the courage to go through before. But my conversation with you made me determined to prove you wrong. Instead, I found a file full of verification. I was wrong and I'm sorry."

Michael remained silent.

"Can you not forgive me?"

"What do you intend to do with the rest of your life?" he asked her.

"Pardon me?"

"The rest of your life ... what do you see happening in it?"

Confused, Sage answered,"my dream is ... my dream is to go back to my people. Preserve their heritage, their art. And now that I have some money, I'd like to invest it in the reservation to be used to teach children the dances, the parables, the arts, and the beliefs of the Zuni."

"What would you say if I told you I have a dream like yours?"

"You have a dream like mine?"

Michael turned to her, and looked as though he would drink her up. "Yes. I have a dream like yours. I tried to get away from you, to get away from the *thought* of you. I went away, to be alone. To get the sliver of you out of my bleeding heart. But you haunted me. I went to a museum, and immediately I encountered a picture of your mother ...."

Sage gasped.

"Yes, I gasped too. It was like looking at you like this, in moonlight. The dark beauty. I'm a fool. A complete and utter fool if I think I can get away from you. I cannot. I love you. That's all. I don't understand this feeling. It makes me miserable. It makes me giddy.

"But the problem is, no matter what I do, I cannot escape it."

It was as if Michael was reading her journal. "Me too," she said simply.

Michael wrapped his arms around her, and she moved to him, the ocean wave drawn to shore. Their long and lingering kiss, *this* particular wave that had been coming up from the depths of the ocean for months—or perhaps, even, years—finally surfaced, sealing an eternal love.

It could be no other way. Sage knew now that no matter how far away from one another they had tried to run, they would run into one another. Love is a circle, and it returns to love.

She buried her face in his fresh-as-spring scent, felt the firm flesh of his chest, heard his heart beating rapidly.

"I'd say, if you have a dream like mine, it's about time you told me." She looked up into his eyes.

Michael kissed a corn flower in one of her braids. "I've been tortured over you."

"And I've had many sleepless nights," Sage answered.

They fell silent, content to finally be in the one place they'd each yearned for since they first met.

"What a waste of time our pride has caused." Michael held her even tighter, breathed her in, deeply. Then he disengaged himself enough to reach into his suit coat pocket. "I have something for you."

"For me? It's *Anthony's* birthday."

"I left my present for him on the table. How different—and wonderful!—tonight has turned out from what I expected. I sincerely thought you and Anthony were going to announce your engagement, I thought that was why you've not talked to me."

"When in fact I haven't talked to you because I wanted to surprise you with Alison."

"And you *did!* Wasn't she glorious when she stepped into the room? How did you make the sun do that? You are truly amazing, Sage. Not only kind and loving, but you know how to put things together so that everyone feels their best." He handed her the box with the Zuni necklace. "When I was at the museum where I saw the picture of your mother, I bought this for you this as an present if you became engaged to Anthony."

Sage opened the box then raised surprised eyes to Michael. "Zuni craftsmanship. You were serious about your life intentions—that they are like mine?"

"Very serious. Very much like yours."

Tears came into Sage's eyes. "Oh, Michael," she whispered. She handed him the necklace so he could clasp it around her throat.

They quietly lingered in one another's arms for a few more moments. Then Sage remembered the party, which had simply faded from her mind. "I suppose I must return to the party."

"I suppose we both must," Michael agreed.

When they reentered the party room, the lights were dimmed. Almost everyone was dancing, a few people stood about, engaged in conversation. Anthony sat in a corner with Alison.

"There you two are!" Anthony exclaimed as Michael and Sage approached him. He paused for a moment, taking in their held hands and the energy between them. "Yes, this is good, you two. Why didn't I—why didn't *you two*—see it before? It seemed as if you were always kind of sparring."

"We were," Michael replied.

"But we—resolved our differences," Sage added.

Michael chuckled and put his arm around her.

"Thank you, Sage," Anthony said. "Thank you for the party. Thank you for bringing Alison."

"Yes, thank you for insisting I come, Sage," Alison agreed.

"I wasn't about to have it any other way," Sage said happily. At that moment, she noticed Millie approaching them. She saw Millie observe Michael's arm around her. She watched as Millie took half a step back, and then her face closed up as if a curtain had drawn across it. She looked quickly away so Millie would not know what she had seen.

"I've been looking all over for you, Michael," Millie chirped coming up to them. She gestured to his arm around Sage. "So, you two finally figured things out?"

"Yes, finally is right," Michael agreed. "I know you tried to tell me, my friend."

Millie shrugged. "Everything happens in due season."

"Lovely quote, who said that?" Michael asked.

"Well, I believe it was me. Just now."

Everyone chuckled.

"Oh, Millie, what would I would have done without you? You're a treasure," Sage said, tucking away the knowledge of Millie's broken heart. She could do no more than she was doing already, providing her a home and an income.

"Well, I'm not going anywhere."

Anthony stood and extended his hand to Alison. "Would you like to dance, my dear?"

"Certainly."

They whirled onto the dance floor, moving as one.

The dowager princess came up to Michael, Sage, and Millie on the arm of a dark, attractive young man. "Sage, I'd like you to meet my grandson, Ernest."

Sage shook his hand, "Nice to meet you, Ernest."

"Nice to meet you, too," he said, but he had his eyes on Millie. "Would you like to dance?"

Millie's eyebrows went up in surprise. "Me?"

"Yes, you." He took her hand and swept her onto the dance floor. The dowager princess shrugged and returned to her music.

Michael and Sage moved slowly to the music that swirled around them, as if their feet might never again touch earth, and yet, more grounded than ever. They exchanged a look that *Time* loved to see … the look beyond words, when two broken hearts become whole as one, in the healing balm of love.

The End

for coming along on a journey on the **Canyon Road**.
To receive a free download of the first chapters
of **One Love** – *Book 2* in the *Canyon Road Love Stories*
series, go to:

http://bit.ly/OneLove-partial

If you'd like the entire book in exchange for
writing a review, send your request to me at:

Thea@EmersonandTilman.com

About The Author...

I'm a full-time writer, creating the worlds in my novels, in the Portland, Oregon area. Having lived in and visited many places around the world, I happily settled in the beautiful Northwest, where the environment and culture are perfect for a writing life. The rain, the forests, the water falls, mountains, and ocean—plus lots of writers—make it a great place to be a writer.

Thank you beforehand for any kind review you may write–which is warmly received and much appreciated! If you have questions or comments, I'd love to hear from you ….

Thea@emersonandtilman.com